MATT AND TOM OLDFIELD

ULTIMATE
FOOTBALL HEROES

WORLD CUP SPECIAL

FROM THE PLAYGROUND
TO THE PITCH

DINO

First published by Dino Books in 2022,
an imprint of Bonnier Books UK,
4th Floor, Victoria House, Bloomsbury Square, London WC1B 4DA
Owned by Bonnier Books,
Sveavägen 56, Stockholm, Sweden

@UFHbooks
@footieheroesbks
www.heroesfootball.com
www.bonnierbooks.co.uk

Paperback ISBN: 978 1 78946 489 4
E-book ISBN: 978 1 78946 497 9

British Library cataloguing-in-publication data:
A catalogue record for this book is available from the British Library.

Printed and bound in Great Britain by Clays Ltd, Elcograf S.p.A.

1 3 5 7 9 10 8 6 4 2

ULTIMATE FOOTBALL HEROES

Matt Oldfield is a children's author focusing on the wonderful world of football. His other books include *Unbelievable Football* (winner of the 2020 Children's Sports Book of the Year) and the *Johnny Ball: Football Genius* series. In association with his writing, Matt also delivers writing workshops in schools.

Cover illustration by Dan Leydon.
To learn more about Dan visit danleydon.com
To purchase his artwork visit etsy.com/shop/footynews
Or just follow him on Twitter @danleydon

TABLE OF CONTENTS

ACKNOWLEDGEMENTS

First of all I'd like to thank everyone at Bonnier Books, especially Saaleh Patel, for supporting me and for running the ever-expanding UFH ship so smoothly. Writing stories for the next generation of football fans is both an honour and a pleasure. Thanks also to my agent, Nick Walters, for helping to keep my dream job going, year after year.

Next up, an extra big cheer for all the teachers, booksellers and librarians who have championed these books, and, of course, for the readers. The success of this series is truly down to you.

Okay, onto friends and family. I wouldn't be writing this series if it wasn't for my brother Tom. I owe him so much and I'm very grateful for his belief in me as an author. I'm also very grateful to the rest of my family, especially Mel, Noah, Nico, and of course Mum and Dad. To my parents, I owe my biggest passions: football and books. They're a real inspiration for everything I do.

Pang, Will, Mills, Doug, Naomi, John, Charlie, Sam, Katy, Ben, Karen, Ana (and anyone else I forgot) – thanks for all the love and laughs, but sorry, no I won't be getting 'a real job' anytime soon!

And finally, I couldn't have done any of this without Iona's encouragement and understanding. Much love to you, and of course to Arlo, the ultimate hero of all. I hope we get to enjoy these books together one day.

KYLIAN
MBAPPÉ

PART 1

FROM RUSSIA WITH LOVE

On 14 July 2018, Kylian sent a message to his millions of social media followers, from Russia with love: 'Happy French national day everyone. Let's hope the party continues until tomorrow night!'

'Tomorrow night' – 15 July – was when the national team would be playing in the 2018 World Cup final at the Luzhniki Stadium in Moscow. It was the most important football match on the planet and Kylian's country was counting on him.

So far, he hadn't let them down at all. In fact, Kylian had been France's speedy superstar, scoring the winning goal against Denmark and then two more goals against Argentina in an amazing man-of-the-match performance. That all made him France's best 'Number 10' since Zinedine Zidane in 1998.

That was the year that France had last won the World Cup.

That was also the year that Kylian was born.

Twenty years on and 'Les Bleus' were the favourites to lift the famous golden trophy again. They had already beaten Lionel Messi's Argentina in the Round of 16, Luis Suárez's Uruguay in the quarter-finals and Kevin De Bruyne's Belgium in the semi-finals. Now, the only nation standing in their way was Luka Modrić's Croatia.

'You've done so well to get this far,' the France manager, Didier Deschamps, told them as kick-off approached and the nerves began to jangle. 'Now, you just need to go out there and finish off the job!'

A massive 'Yeah!' echoed around the room. It was one big team effort, from captain Hugo Lloris in goal through to Kylian, Antoine Griezmann and Olivier Giroud in attack. Everyone worked hard and everyone worked together.

If others' nerves were jangling, though, Kylian

stayed calm. He was the coolest character around, and never let anything faze him. When he was younger, he hadn't just hoped to play in a World Cup final; he had expected it. It was all part of his killer plan to conquer the football world.

Out on the pitch in Moscow, Kylian sang the French national anthem with a big smile on his face. As a four-year-old, some people had laughed at his ambitious dreams. Well, they definitely weren't laughing now.

'Right, let's do this!' Paul Pogba clapped and cheered as they took up their positions. His partnership with Kylian would be key for France. Whenever Paul got the ball in midfield, he would look to find his pacy teammate with a perfect pass.

Kylian's first action of the final, however, was in defence. He rushed back quickly to block a Croatia cross.

'Well done!' France's centre-back Samuel Umtiti shouted.

Once that was done, it was all about attacking. Even in a World Cup final, Kylian wasn't afraid to try his tricks and flicks. They didn't always work but it was worth the risk.

It was an end-to-end first half, full of action. First, Antoine curled in a dangerous free kick and Mario Mandžukić headed the ball into his own net: 1–0 to France! Kylian punched the air – what a start! Ivan Perišić equalised for Croatia but then he handballed it in his own box. Penalty! Antoine stepped up... and scored: 2–1 to France!

The French players were happy to hear the half-time whistle. They needed a break to regroup. Although they were winning, they had work to do if they wanted to become world champions again.

'We need to calm things down and take control of the game,' Deschamps told his players. 'Stay smart out there!'

Kylian listened carefully to his manager's message. He needed to relax and play to his strengths – his skill but also his speed. This was his chance to go down in World Cup history:

Pelé in 1958,

Diego Maradona in 1986,

Zidane in 1998,

Ronaldo in 2002,

Kylian in 2018?

In the second-half, France's superstars shone more brightly. Kylian collected Paul's long pass and sprinted straight past the Croatia centre-back. Was he about to score in his first World Cup final? No, the keeper came out to make a good save.

'Ohhhh!' the supporters groaned in disappointment.

But a few minutes later, Paul and Kylian linked up again. From wide on the right wing, Kylian dribbled towards goal. Uh-oh, the Croatia left-back was in big trouble.

With a stepover and a little hop, Kylian cut inside towards goal but in a flash, he fooled the defender with another quick change of direction.

'Go on!' the France fans urged their exciting young hero.

What next? Kylian still had two defenders in front of him, so he pulled it back to Antoine instead. He couldn't find a way through either, so he passed to Paul. Paul's first shot was blocked but his second flew into the bottom corner. 3–1!

Kylian threw his arms up in the air and then ran over to congratulate his friend. Surely, France had one hand on the World Cup trophy now.

Antoine had scored, and now so had Paul. That meant it must be Kylian's turn next! He would have to score soon, however, in case Deschamps decided to take him off early…

When he received the pass from Lucas Hernández, Kylian was in the middle of the pitch, at least ten yards outside the penalty area. Was he too far out to shoot? No, there was no such thing as 'too far' for Kylian! He shifted the ball to the right and then BANG! He tucked the ball into the bottom corner before the keeper could even dive. *4–1!*

Goooooooooooooooooooooaaaaaaaaaaaaaaaaalllllllllllllll llllllllllll!!!!!!!!!!!!!!!!!!!!

As his teammates rushed over to him, Kylian had just enough time for his trademark celebration. With a little jump, he planted his feet, folded his arms across his chest, and tried to look as cool as he could. That last part was really hard, because he had just scored in a World Cup final!

The next thirty minutes ticked by very slowly but eventually, the game was over. France 4 Croatia 2 – they were the 2018 World Champions!

Allez Les Bleus! Allez Les Bleus! Allez Les Bleus!

Kylian used the last of his energy to race around the pitch, handing out hugs to everyone he saw: his sad opponents, his happy teammates, his manager, EVERYONE! In that amazing moment, he would have hugged every single French person in the world if he could. Instead, he blew kisses at the cameras. From Russia with love!

And Kylian's incredible night wasn't over yet. Wearing his country's flag around his waist, he walked up on stage to collect the tournament's Best Young Player award from Emmanuel Macron.

'Thank you, you're a national hero now!' the French President told him proudly.

'My pleasure, Sir!' Kylian replied.

Would Kylian's smile ever fade? Certainly not while he had a World Cup winners' medal around his neck and the beautiful World Cup trophy in his hands. He didn't ever want to let go. He kissed it and raised it high into the Moscow night sky.

'Hurray!' the fans cheered for him.

At the age of nineteen, Kylian was already living out his wildest dreams. The boy from Bondy had become a World Cup winner and football's next great superstar.

PART 2

FROM (FRANCE) HERO TO ZERO

28 June 2021, National Arena, Romania

For their Euro 2020 Round of 16 clash with Switzerland, the France team walked out onto the pitch in position order. Captain and goalkeeper Hugo Lloris led the way, followed by the defenders, then the midfielders, and finally the new and improved all-star attack. As if Kylian and Antoine weren't amazing enough already, France now had striker Karim Benzema back too. Wow, no wonder they were the favourites to win the Euros, as well as the World Cup!

Kylian wasn't getting carried away, though; no, he

wasn't that kind of character. Instead, he was staying calm and taking the tournament step by step, match by match:

A 1–0 win over Germany,

A 1–1 draw with Hungary,

A 2–2 draw with Portugal…

…and next, hopefully another win against Switzerland in the Round of 16.

After Kylian's wonderful 2018 World Cup and another superb season for his club, PSG, he had arrived at Euro 2020 with great expectations. So far, things hadn't really clicked for him, but there were encouraging signs of improvement. Although he still hadn't scored a goal himself, he had won a penalty against Portugal with one of his bursting runs into the box, and played well against his boyhood hero, Cristiano Ronaldo.

Now, in the knockout stages, it was Kylian's time to really shine. Out on the left wing, he somehow managed to weave his way past five opponents and deliver a cross into the box. It was curling right towards Karim at the back post, but at the last second, a defender booted it away for a corner.

'Great ball!' his strike partner applauded.

But just as Kylian was getting up to full speed and into the game, Switzerland took a surprise lead. Steven Zuber whipped a great ball into the middle and Haris Seferović angled his header brilliantly down into the bottom corner. 1–0!

Wow, the underdogs were winning! For now. Kylian was determined to be France's comeback kid, but in the first half, he was missing his usual bit of magic.

He attempted to lay the ball across to Karim, but his pass landed too far in front of him.

He almost escaped from the last Swiss defender, but his first touch was too heavy and the ball rolled through to the keeper.

'Arghhhhhh!' Kylian cried out, throwing his hands to his head. What an opportunity!

As the game went on, he grew more and more desperate to make a difference. He smashed a free kick straight into the Switzerland wall, and sliced the rebound way wide. Then just before half-time, he blazed a shot high over the bar.

'ARGHHHHHH!' What was going on?

It took a while for France to find their best form, but eventually in the second half, their attackers came alive. Antoine poked the ball through to Kylian, who this time managed to pick out Karim with a pass. 1–1!

'That's more like it!' Kylian thought to himself, punching the air with both fists. At last, France were back in the game, and soon, they seemed to be cruising towards the quarter-finals.

Antoine passed to Kylian, who backheeled it back for the one-two. Olé! Antoine was into the box now, and he chipped a cross to Karim at the back post. 2–1!

It was a beautiful goal, and so was the third, a long-range strike from Paul that curled into the top corner. 3–1!

That should have been game over, but France made the mistake of switching off and Switzerland took full advantage. First, Seferović scored a second header and then in the very last minute, Mario

Gavranović fired in an excellent equaliser. 3–3!

Kylian couldn't believe it – from 3–1 up, now the game was going to extra-time! Oh well, at least it was another chance for him to be France's hero. It had to be him, and in the 110th minute, his golden opportunity arrived. Paul guided the ball in between the Swiss defenders, putting Kylian one-on-one with the keeper. Surely, he had to score this time, but no – at the crucial moment, he slipped and sliced his shot past the post.

Noooooooooo!

What? How? Why? No-one quite knew, but Kylian had wasted France's best and last chance to score a winner, and so the match went all the way to penalties.

The tension was rising all around the stadium, but standing on the halfway line, Kylian watched with his teammates as player after player walked calmly forward and scored:

Gavranović, Fabian Schär, Manuel Akanji, and Rubén Vargas for Switzerland...

...and Paul, Olivier Giroud, Marcus Thuram, and

Presnel Kimpembe for France.

It was 4–4! Would Admir Mehmedi be the first to miss? No, he calmly sent Lloris the wrong way, putting all the pressure on France's fifth penalty-taker... Kylian!

Yes, he was still young and his shooting had been pretty bad during the match, but he was a player born for these big-game moments. Approaching the spot, he looked as cool as ever. He placed the ball down and then waited for the referee's whistle.

'Of course, he's going to score,' the France supporters believed.

After a short run-up, Kylian pulled his right leg back and whipped the ball to the left. He was aiming for the top corner, but instead his shot flew much lower than that, at the perfect height for Yann Sommer's strong left hand. SAVED!

NOOOOOOOO!

Kylian turned away in despair and threw his hands to his head, while the Swiss players sprinted past him to celebrate with their keeper. It was all over; his penalty miss meant that France, the tournament favourites, were out of Euro 2020.

He trudged around the pitch in a daze. His teammates tried their best to comfort him, but nothing they said could change the reality. He had just gone from a World Cup hero in 2018 to a Euro villain in 2021.

'I am sorry for this penalty,' Kylian posted on social media the morning after the match. 'I wanted to help the team but I failed... I know that you, the fans, are disappointed, but I would still like to thank you for your support and always believing in us. The most important thing is to come back even stronger next time.'

PART 3

BACK TO HIS BEST (IN THE NATIONS LEAGUE)

Football moved too fast for Kylian to stay down for long. Just three months after his Euro disappointment, he was challenging for another trophy with France in the UEFA Nations League finals. This time, it was just a two-match tournament:

A semi-final against Belgium…

…and then if they beat them, a final against either Spain or Italy.

'Right, let's win this!' Kylian told his teammates. It wouldn't be easy against such tough opponents, but this was his chance to bounce straight back with goals and glory, and he was determined to take it.

At half-time against Belgium, however, France were

2–0 down and falling apart. Where was the usual strength in defence, the energy in midfield, and the creativity in attack?

'That was nowhere near good enough!' Deschamps screamed at his players, breaking the stony silence in the dressing room. 'But luckily, this game isn't over yet – we've still got forty-five minutes to turn things around, so go out there and do it.'

It was the wake-up call that France really needed. As the second half went on, *Les Bleus* got better and better. Paul began to control the game with his passing, Antoine was getting crosses into the box, and Kylian was causing all kinds of problems for the Belgium defence.

With a stepover and a body swerve, Kylian skipped straight past Yannick Carrasco on the right and sprinted into the penalty area. After a quick look up, he then crossed the ball to Antoine, but his shot bobbled just wide. So close!

Never mind, Kylian was in the groove now. Three minutes later, he popped up on the left, winning the ball off Kevin De Bruyne and then fooling Youri

Tielemans with his fancy footwork. Again, he looked up and picked out a teammate in the middle. This time, it was Karim, who turned and fired a shot past Thibaut Courtois. 2–1!

Game on! Kylian grabbed the ball out of the net and carried it back to the halfway line for the restart. He was on fire and France had more goals to get…

Before Belgium knew it, Kylian was dribbling into the box again at speed. His shot deflected away off a defender, but as Antoine chased after it, Tielemans appeared to trip him up.

'Penalty!' cried Kylian, along with every France player and fan. Eventually, after a long VAR check, it was given.

So, who would take it? Karim? Antoine? No, despite his painful miss at Euro 2020, Kylian was the one who put the ball down on the spot. And this time, he aimed for the top corner and found it with an unstoppable strike. *2–2!*

Goooooooooooooooooooooooaaaaaaaaaaaaaaaaaaallllllllllllllllllllllllllllll!!!!!!!!!!!!!!!!!!!!!!

Kylian raced towards the corner flag with his arms

out wide, feeling on top of the world. He was back – back to his best!

'Woooooooooooooo!' he cried out, as he stood in front of the France fans with his arms folded across his chest, showing off his trademark celebration.

Now, who would be the matchwinner?

De Bruyne? No, Hugo tipped his fizzing strike over the bar.

Antoine? No, his blast was blocked by a Belgium defender.

Kylian? After a lovely one-two with Karim, he cut back onto his right foot and chipped a shot towards the corner of the net, but it whistled just past the post.

'Ooooooooohhhh!' he gasped, putting his hands to his face.

Romelu Lukaku? He guided the ball into the net, but the goal was ruled out for offside.

Paul? No, his free kick clipped the top of the crossbar.

What an entertaining, end-to-end match! Just when it seemed destined for extra-time, an unlikely hero stepped forward with a fantastic winning goal for

France: left-back Theo Hernández.

'Yesssssssssssssssss!' Kylian yelled, racing over to jump on his teammate. They had done it; the comeback was complete, and France were through to the Nations League final.

'Great work from the whole team. See you on Sunday!!!!!' Kylian tweeted happily. 'ALLEZ LES BLEUS!'

When Sunday arrived, France started the final brilliantly. Their attackers were linking up beautifully all over the pitch: Paul to Antoine to Karim to Kylian. The only thing missing was a goal. Spain grew stronger as the game went on, but at half-time, at least the France players knew their manager would be much happier with their performance so far.

'Just keep playing the same way,' Deschamps told them in the dressing room. 'The goals will come.'

He was right, they did – but unfortunately, the first one went to Spain. Moments after Theo had cracked a shot against the crossbar at one end, Mikel Oyarzabal dribbled through and scored at the other. 1–0!

Oh well – to win the final, France would just have

to fight back again, like they had against Belgium. And they did, almost instantly…

Antoine flicked the ball on to Paul, who spread it left to Kylian, who passed it on to Karim. From a wide angle on the edge of the penalty area, he somehow curled an incredible shot into the top corner. 1–1!

'Woaahhh!' Kylian screamed out in disbelief as he threw his arms around his strike partner. What an unbelievable goal to score in such a big game!

Now, who would be the matchwinner this time? Kylian was determined to become a French football hero again.

He tried an ambitious chip from outside the box, but the ball flew high over the bar.

Then he got a touch on Antoine's cross, but not enough to beat the Spain keeper.

Ooooooooohh, nearly – Kylian was getting closer…

With ten minutes to go, he made a classic striker's run in between the centre-backs to reach Theo's brilliant through-ball.

'Offside!' cried the Spain defenders in desperation, but the flag stayed down. Uh-oh – they were in big trouble now.

When he entered the box, Kylian slowed down and kept himself calm. This was a golden opportunity, and he wasn't going to waste it, not like he had in extra-time against Switzerland at the Euros. So, what was the plan? As Unai Simón came rushing out towards him, Kylian faked to shoot with his right foot, but after a stylish stepover, he hit it with his left instead, giving the keeper no chance.

Goooooooooooooooooooooaaaaaaaaaaaaaaaaalllllllllllllll llllllllllllll!!!!!!!!!!!!!!!!!!!!

It was 2–1 to France! After watching to make sure the ball rolled into the net, Kylian turned and raced over to the corner. He was so excited that he jumped over the advertising boards to get even closer to the fans.

'Yessssss, you did it, you did it!' Theo shouted in his ear as they celebrated together.

Hugo had a few more saves to make first, but eventually, the final whistle blew. France were the 2021 UEFA Nations League Winners, and Kylian was their comeback hero! With a huge smile on his face, he raised both arms high into the air like the champion he was. It felt so good to be back – back to his best.

PART 4

FIRING FRANCE TO QATAR

The next challenge for Kylian and his national teammates was qualifying for the big one: the 2022 World Cup. As the reigning champions, France had been expected to cruise their way to Qatar, but with two games to go, they were just three points ahead of Ukraine, and four ahead of Finland, at the top of Group D. Only the team in first place would go straight through to the tournament, and so they still needed one more win to secure a World Cup spot as they kicked off against bottom-of-the-table Kazakhstan at the Stade de France in Paris.

After missing the last two qualifiers through injury, Kylian was back – back to his best – to help finish the job for *Les Bleus*. In fact, he gave France the lead in the fifth minute, at the end of another awesome team attack. The move started with Antoine, who passed it across to Karim, who slipped it through to Theo as he raced up the left wing on an overlapping run. Looking up, he spotted Kylian on the sprint, and when the cross came in, he used his side-foot to carefully guide the ball into the bottom corner. 1–0!

'Come onnnnnn!' he cried out, thanking Theo with a hug.

It was Kylian's twentieth goal for his country already, and he was only just getting started. Six minutes later, he scored again. 2–0!

'Yessssssssssss!' he cheered joyfully as he jumped into the arms of Kingsley Coman, the winger who had set him up. He was very lucky to have so many talented and unselfish teammates around him.

Right, could Kylian now successfully complete a first-half hat-trick? Of course, he could! He even did it with thirteen minutes to spare. As another accurate cross from Kingsley flew towards him, he jumped up and flicked a powerful header into the far corner of the net. 3–0!

Game over – France were surely on their way to the World Cup now! 'Hurray!' the home crowd cheered, as Kylian and his teammates really got the party going.

Karim tapped in after more great work from Theo. 4–0!

Kylian got another great chance to score, but instead, kindly slid the ball across to Karim. 5–0!

Adrien Rabiot headed in from a corner. 6–0!

Antoine fired in from the penalty spot. 7–0!

And then Kylian finished things off with his fourth of the game. 8–0!

With each goal their team scored, the fans in the stands waved their French flags a little harder and higher, creating a beautiful sea of blue, white and red.

Wow, what a way to qualify for Qatar! At the end of a truly memorable match, Kylian walked proudly off the pitch with the ball tucked under his arm, while also holding up four fingers for the cameras, one for each of his goals.

France still had a trip to Finland to go, but the

players refused to relax and treat it like a pointless game. Every match mattered, especially when there were great goals to set up and score...

When Karim passed the ball through to Kylian in the crowded penalty area, he skilfully flicked it back for his strike partner to shoot. 1–0!

'Thanks, you're the best!' Karim shouted as he raced over to celebrate. They were quickly becoming international football's most dangerous duo.

Ten minutes later, Kylian collected a pass near the halfway line and ZOOM! He was off, leaving the Finland defenders trailing behind. In a flash, he was into the box, where he curled the ball into the far corner. 2–0!

Goooooooooooooooooooooaaaaaaaaaaaaaaaaalllllllllllllllll llllllllllll!!!!!!!!!!!!!!!!!!!

On the run like that, Kylian looked simply unstoppable! Brazil, Argentina, Belgium, England – how would the other top teams at the 2022 World Cup cope with his super-speed and skill?

KEVIN
DE BRUYNE

PART 1

BELGIUM'S HISTORY-MAKING HEROES

On the same day that France took on Croatia in the 2018 World Cup final in Moscow, another football celebration was taking place outside the Royal Palace in Brussels. That's because with a 2–0 play-off win over England, the Belgium team had officially finished in third place, their best-ever performance at a World Cup tournament.

History made! Such an amazing achievement called for a proper party. The Grand Place was packed with thousands of proud supporters, all dressed in the colours of the Belgium flag: black, yellow and red. And after a special congratulations from King Philippe and Queen Mathilde, the twenty-three members of the national squad made their way, one by one, out onto the balcony to be welcomed home as heroes.

Team captain Eden Hazard led the way, wearing sunglasses and a backwards-baseball cap, and he soon got the fans singing and dancing in the streets.

Next came striker Romelu Lukaku, Belgium's top scorer at the World Cup with four goals…

…then Dries Mertens, the clever forward who had kicked things off against Panama…

…and then Kevin, their midfield maestro and matchwinner in the quarter-final against Brazil.

Off the football pitch, he wasn't a natural entertainer like Eden, but with his eyes hidden behind sunglasses and a shy smile on his face, he waved to the Belgium supporters below and then slowly raised both arms up in the air. 'Ooooooooooooh…'

'…Hurrrraaaaaaaaaaaaaayyyyy!' the fans cheered back.

Two years on from the disappointment of losing to Wales in the quarter-finals of Euro 2016, at last Belgium's Golden Generation had lived up to their great expectations. But while Kevin was glad to give the nation something to cheer about, he couldn't help wondering 'What if':

What if Eden had finished off the chance that Kevin had created for him in the first half of the semi-final against France?

What if Kevin himself had hit the target in the seventy-fifth minute, rather than slicing his shot high over the crossbar?

And what if, with time running out, Romelu had got his head to Kevin's incredible cross-field pass?

Oh well, that was football; a single moment could make all the difference. Kevin was still only twenty-seven and so was Eden, while Romelu was just twenty-five. They still had lots of time, and lots more major tournaments together, starting with Euro 2020 and the 2022 World Cup.

Kevin was determined to help his country qualify for both tournaments, but unfortunately, he was forced to miss a lot of Belgium's matches due to a series of injuries at Manchester City. First, he tore a knee ligament, then he hurt his thigh, and then he twisted his ankle.

Noooooooooooo!

Even so, in the few games that he was able to play, Kevin showed that he was still the King of the Assists.

He set up three and scored the fourth goal himself in a Euros qualifier against Scotland...

...added two more assists against Russia...

...and then one more against Cyprus, as well as two goals of his own.

Job done; with ten wins out of ten, Belgium were off to Euro 2020! 'To be continued...' Kevin tweeted with excitement. He couldn't wait, but in the end, he had to because the tournament was delayed by one year due to the coronavirus pandemic. That meant that their road to the 2022 World Cup actually began before the Euros had even taken place. It was all quite confusing, but the only thing Kevin cared about was winning each and every game.

Belgium kicked off their World Cup qualification campaign against Wales, who took an early lead at the Den Dreef Stadium in Leuven. Luckily, however, Kevin was fully fit this time and ready to lead the Belgian fightback. First, he almost set up Romelu with a sensational cross, and then five minutes later, he went for goal himself, whipping a swerving shot into the bottom corner. *1–1!*

Goooooooooooooooooooooaaaaaaaaaaaaaaaaallllllllllllll llllllllll!!!!!!!!!!!!!!!!!!!!

'Yesssssss, Kev!' shouted Toby Alderweireld, who wasn't even surprised by his teammate's wonderstrike. He'd seen him do it so many times before, in training and in matches.

From there, Belgium went on to beat Wales 3–1, but three days later, they found themselves 1–0 down again, this time away against the Czech Republic. Uh-oh – a defeat would be a disaster, especially so early in the World Cup qualification campaign. Could they turn things around like they had against Wales? With Eden out injured, there was even more pressure on Belgium's two other top superstars to save the day...

Ten minutes after the Czech goal, Kevin collected the ball in the centre-circle, turned, took a quick look around and then slid a perfectly-weighted pass through to Romelu. They had been playing together for so long that they knew what the other would do without even thinking. In the penalty area, Romelu escaped from the last defender and slammed a shot through the keeper's legs. 1–1!

Phew! While Romelu ran over to grab the ball out of the net, the other Belgium players went over to congratulate Kevin on yet another amazing assist. What would they do without him?

Unfortunately, that worst fear became a reality again because just days before the Belgium squad met up to prepare for Euro 2020, Kevin suffered another bad injury. In the Champions League final, he tried to play a one-two with his Manchester City teammate Riyad Mahrez, but as he turned, BAM! He barely remembered the next part, but his face had smacked straight into the shoulder of Chelsea defender Antonio Rüdiger.

Argghhhhhhhhhhh!

Both players fell to the floor, but only Rüdiger was able to carry on. Kevin, meanwhile, hobbled off the pitch in tears and was rushed straight to hospital, where the news wasn't good: he had fractured his nose and one of his eye sockets.

Nooooooooooooooo!

That sounded serious – how long would he be out for? While Kevin's club season was already over, the race was now on to be fit in time to play for his country at Euro 2020...

PART 2

A FRUSTRATING EUROS TO FORGET

Just one week after that painful Champions League final, Kevin arrived in a town called Tubize, Belgium's base camp for Euro 2020. 'Hurray!' the whole nation cheered with joy and relief.

He wasn't yet able to train properly with his teammates, though, so instead, he followed his own special solo programme, working hard to be ready to play at least some part in the tournament. His country was counting on him.

In the end, Kevin did have to miss Belgium's first match, a tricky trip to Russia, but the 'Red Devils' managed to get the job done without their midfield maestro. Romelu grabbed two goals and right wing-back Thomas Meunier scored the other.

'Well done, guys!' Kevin congratulated his teammates after the win. Belgium now had a five-day break before their second group match against Denmark, and he was hoping that his facial injuries would have healed by then.

Kevin started the game on the subs bench, and the plan was to wait and just let him play the last fifteen or twenty minutes. But with Denmark winning 1–0, the Belgium manager Roberto Martínez decided to bring him on at half-time. They needed him now!

It didn't take long for Kevin to change the game; less than ten minutes, in fact. From the middle of the pitch, he swept a quick, first-time pass out to Romelu on the right wing, and then kept running towards the box for the return ball.

'Yes, Rom!'

When it arrived, Kevin faked to shoot but then calmly shifted the ball further to the right instead, fooling the two Danish defenders in front of him, who dived to the floor. What now? 'Shoot!' cried the Belgium supporters behind the goal, but no, Kevin unselfishly slid the ball across to Eden's brother, Thorgan Hazard, for a tap-in. *1–1!*

'Thanks, mate – you're the best!' Thorgan shouted as they high-fived together. Then they rushed straight back to the halfway line to begin hunting for a second, winning goal.

It arrived fifteen minutes later, and who was Belgium's matchwinner? Yes, you guessed it – Kevin! He followed up his amazing assist with an equally great goal of his own.

With Denmark defending deep, Belgium moved the ball swiftly from right to left – Romelu to Youri Tielemans, to Thorgan, to Eden, to Kevin, who fired off a low left-foot strike that flew into the bottom corner. *2–1!*

Gooooooooooooooooooooaaaaaaaaaaaaaaaaaalllllllllllllll lllllllllllll!!!!!!!!!!!!!!!!!!!!!

Kevin was back with a bang – what a big difference he made to the Belgium team! Jogging over to the corner flag, he threw his arms out wide and then waved his hands towards the ground as if to calm the fans down. There was no need to fear, now that he was here.

With two wins out of two, The Red Devils were already through to the Euro 2020 Last 16 – wouldn't it be a good idea for Kevin to rest ahead of the knockout rounds? No, he wanted more game-time first, and so Martínez let him play ninety minutes in their last group match against Finland. Again, Kevin was Belgium's star man and the best player on the pitch, setting up both goals with a dangerous corner-kick and then a clever poked pass through to Romelu.

'Yesssss, bro!' the striker cheered as they did their classic celebration. They had played so many international matches together, and scored so many goals – what a deadly duo they were!

After one-and-a-half games back in the Belgium team, Kevin now felt ready and raring to go for their Last 16 superstar clash with Cristiano Ronaldo's Portugal. It was all set to be a brilliant battle between two top teams, but at half-time, it was Belgium who had the lead, thanks to a swerving thunderbolt from Thorgan.

'Come onnnnn!' Kevin roared as he chased over to

celebrate with his teammates. In the knockout rounds at major tournaments, every goal was massive. Yes, it was so far so good for the Red Devils, but early in the second half, disaster struck. No, Portugal didn't equalise; Kevin picked up yet another injury.

Nooooooooooo!

This time, it was his ankle, which he'd hurt in a tackle with João Palhinha in the first half. Kevin had tried his best to bravely play on through the pain, but eventually it became clear that he just couldn't carry on. If he did, his tournament would be over, so he hobbled slowly off the field, shaking his head, and Dries ran on to replace him.

Without their best playmaker, Belgium didn't score again, but their defence stayed strong until the very end. 1–0 – they were through to the Euro quarter-finals again!

'Staying a little longer,' Kevin tweeted afterwards, but the big question was: would he be fit in time to face Italy?

Fortunately for Belgium, the answer turned out to

be yes, although he had to have horrible painkilling injections in order to play. And as hard as he tried out on the pitch, Kevin just couldn't produce his usual midfield magic.

He unleashed a powerful shot from the edge of the penalty area, but the ball didn't fly into the bottom corner like normal. *SAVED!*

Instead, Italy went up the other end and took a two-goal lead. Romelu pulled one goal back from the penalty spot just before half-time, but still, Belgium were in big trouble. What could Kevin do to save the day?

After the break, he attempted to pick out Romelu with lots of clever passes, but none of them quite reached their target. *INTERCEPTED!*

'Arghhhhhh!' Kevin cried out, growing more and more frustrated. If only he was fully fit; it would be a totally different story for Belgium.

He wasn't going to give up, though. In the final moments of the match, Kevin raced onto Jérémy Doku's throughball and delivered a perfect cross towards Romelu in the middle. Surely, he had to equalise and take the match to extra-time, but no, an Italian defender managed to clear it off the goal line. *BLOCKED!*

Sadly, it just wasn't meant to be for Belgium. At the final whistle, Kevin walked around the pitch with his hands on his hips, staring down at the grass below his boots. Losing important football matches was still the worst feeling ever, but at least now Kevin was experienced enough to move on quickly to the next challenge...

PART 3

NEARLY IN THE NATIONS LEAGUE

7 October 2021, Allianz Stadium, Italy

'Come on lads, let's do this!' Kevin clapped and cheered as the Belgian national anthem ended and the players prepared for kick-off. It felt so good to be back in action for his country, especially after his ankle injury from Euro 2020 had kept him out of Belgium's last three World Cup qualifiers. His teammates had won three out of three without him, but there was no way Kevin was missing this big match: the UEFA Nations League semi-final against France.

The top ranked team in the world versus the reigning World Champions – what a mouth-watering clash! Not only that but it was also a repeat of the 2018 World Cup semi-final, which France had won 1–0. So, who would be the winners this time, and make it through to face Spain or Italy in the Nations League final?

Kevin was hungry for revenge, and he almost opened the scoring after just three minutes. Romelu's cross from the right flicked off a French defender and bounced up right in front of Kevin. The ball was at an awkward height to strike, so he lifted his right leg up high and tried to fire it down into the bottom corner, but Hugo Lloris stretched out his left arm and made an excellent save.

'Oooooooooooooooohhhhhhhh!' groaned the Belgium fans behind the goal. What a brilliant start that would have been! Although Kevin was disappointed, he didn't show it. He just got straight on with the game, trying to find another way to win it for his country...

Thirty-five minutes later, Kevin skipped away from Adrien Rabiot in midfield and then passed the ball wide to Yannick Carrasco on the left wing. He dribbled into the box, cut inside on his right foot and fired a surprise shot that beat Lloris at his near post. *1–0!*

'Yesssssss!' Kevin yelled as he ran over to hug Yannick.

They were beating the World Champions, and three minutes later, things got even better for Belgium. Again, it was Kevin who set the goal up, threading a beautiful pass through to Romelu on the right, who spun past his marker and smashed a shot into the roof of the net. *2–0!*

'Come onnnnnn!' Romelu roared, bumping chests with Kevin by the corner flag. Another game, another great goal scored together!

The Red Devils were now in a fantastic position to go on and reach the Nations League final. In the second half, they just had to stay calm and defend well, but against France's all-star attack, that was no simple task...

First, Kylian Mbappé fed the ball to Karim Benzema in the box. *2–1!*

Then Mbappé scored from the penalty spot after a

dodgy foul on Antoine Griezmann. *2–2!*

All of a sudden, the semi-final was tied again! So, which team would go on and win it now? The last twenty minutes were packed with thrilling, end-to-end excitement.

Belgium attacked first, with Romelu laying the ball back to Kevin on the edge of the area. BANG! His rocket of a shot looked like it was heading for the top corner, but up leapt Lloris to tip it over the crossbar.

'Argghhhh!' Kevin snarled angrily, showing some emotion this time. He had so nearly just become Belgium's Nations League hero.

Then forward came France. Benjamin Pavard delivered a great cross to Griezmann in the middle, but Jan Vertonghen blocked his shot, and then Thibaut Courtois saved from Aurélien Tchouaméni. Phew!

In the eighty-sixth minute, seconds after Mbappé had whipped a shot just wide of Courtois's post, Romelu thought he had won it for the Red Devils. But wait, no, VAR were checking the goal, and the verdict was... OFFSIDE!

Noooooooooooo!

It was a crushing blow for the tired Belgium players and it also gave France fresh hope of victory. First, Paul Pogba clipped the top of the crossbar with a curling free kick, and then moments later, the ball fell to Theo Hernández on the left, who fired a stunning shot past Thibaut. 3–2 to France!

Game over – noooooo, not again! For Kevin and his teammates, it was another bitterly disappointing, big-game defeat. Two quarter-final exits at the Euros, a loss in the World Cup semi-finals, and now one in the Nations League too – it felt like Belgium's Golden Generation would never make it through to a major final.

Oh well, it was all about the road to the 2022 World Cup now.

PART 4

QUALIFIED FOR QATAR!

One more win – that's all Belgium needed now to book their place at the 2022 World Cup. Could they get it in their next home game against Estonia? Kevin was feeling very confident as he walked out onto the pitch at the King Baudouin Stadium in Brussels. For once, there was no Romelu in the team, but the Red Devils had plenty of other goalscorers in their squad, plus one of the best midfield playmakers in the world.

In the tenth minute of the match, Kevin dropped deep to collect the ball from the Belgium right-back, Timothy Castagne, and then turned and looked up for a teammate to pass to. Axel Witsel was only a few metres away in central midfield and Thomas Meunier was in space to his right, but instead, Kevin picked out Yannick on the left with a perfect long, diagonal ball. Wow, his accuracy was astonishing! Yannick then delivered a dangerous cross into the box for Christian Benteke to tap in. *1–0* – Belgium were on their way to the World Cup!

In the second half, Yannick scored an excellent second goal, and then Kevin secured the victory by chipping a beautiful cross to the back post for Thorgan to head home. *3–1!*

As the Belgium supporters clapped and danced in the stands, all the Belgium players ran over to congratulate Kevin on another amazing assist.

'Unbelievable ball, mate!' cheered Christian.

'You're a genius!' Dries said with a smile.

With ten minutes to go, Kevin's wonderful work was done, and he left the field to a loud ovation. As soon as the final whistle blew, however, he ran back on in his big black jacket to join in the team celebrations. The Red Devils had done it.

'World Cup, here we come!'

After lots of hugs and high-fives, the players formed

a line in front of the fans and threw their arms in the air together, as gold confetti filled the air.

Hurraaaaaaaaay!

Hurraaaaaaaaay!

Later that night, Kevin shared a special Belgium team poster on social media. Above the words 'QUALIFIED, FIFA WORLD CUP 2022' were photos of all of the players, and who was at the very top, even higher and bigger than those of Eden and Romelu? Yes, Kevin, of course! He was their number one superstar now.

Before they could start preparing for Qatar, though, Belgium still had one more qualifying game to play, away against Wales. With Eden and Jan both missing, Kevin had the honour of wearing the captain's armband, and in the twelfth minute, he made a great day even better by curling a shot into the bottom corner. *1–0!*

Goooooooooooooooooooaaaaaaaaaaaaaaaalllllllllllllll llllllllllll!!!!!!!!!!!!!!!!!!!

While the Belgium fans chanted his name, Kevin stood in front of them with his arms out wide and a proud smile on his face. What a feeling!

In the end, the match finished in a 1–1 draw, but the result didn't really matter that much to Kevin. What mattered was playing for his country at the World Cup, and thanks to his goals and assists, Belgium had achieved that aim.

The tournament was still a whole year away, though, so for now, Kevin switched his focus back to starring for his club. Manchester City were on an ambitious quest to win the quadruple, but one by one, the trophies slipped away...

In the League Cup, Kevin scored the first goal when they thrashed Wycombe Wanderers 6–1 in the third round, but they couldn't find a way past West Ham in the fourth. Kevin was taken off in the eighty-third minute and he watched from the sidelines as his team lost the penalty shoot-out.

Noooooooooo!

In the FA Cup, Kevin set up goals for Gabriel Jesus against Swindon Town, and then John Stones and Riyad Mahrez against Fulham, before scoring one of his own against Southampton. But when it came to the semi-final against Liverpool, Pep Guardiola decided to leave Kevin on the bench, and surprise, surprise, City lost without him.

Noooooooooo!

In the Champions League, Kevin scored the winner against Atlético Madrid in the quarters, and another in the semis against Real, but just when they looked certain to reach the final, City collapsed and conceded three late goals. And where was Kevin as his team were knocked out? Back on the bench after being subbed off.

Noooooooooo!

Kevin couldn't believe it – what on earth had just happened? There was now only one trophy left for City to win: the Premier League title. Surely they couldn't lose that too! Kevin was a midfielder on a mission. He got the winning goal against Chelsea, two more against local rivals Manchester United, and then four against Wolves. And those were just the goals he scored himself; he also set up eight more for his teammates, including the most important goal of all...

Heading into the final day of the season, City sat

just one point above Liverpool at the top of the table. If they could win against Aston Villa, the title would be theirs, but after seventy minutes, they found themselves 2–0 down. Uh-oh, were they about to throw away another trophy?

No – Kevin wasn't going to let that happen, and neither were his City teammates. With time running out, they launched an amazing fightback in the space of just five minutes.

First, super sub İlkay Gündoğan came on and headed home Raheem Sterling's cross. *2–1!*

Then Oleksandr Zinchenko laid the ball across to Rodri, who calmly placed a side-foot shot in the bottom corner. *2–2!*

'Come onnnnnnn!' Kevin roared as the Etihad Stadium erupted. One more goal; that's all they needed now…

Tyrone Mings intercepted João Cancelo's pass and rolled the ball towards his Villa teammate Douglas Luiz, but Kevin raced forward, determined to get there first. With one silky touch, he skipped past the Brazilian and into the box. What next? Without even looking up, Kevin whipped a dangerous ball across the six-yard box, like he had done so many times before. So often, it led to a City goal, but would it work now, when they needed it most?

The fans held their breath as the ball flew past each Villa defender, and all the way through to İlkay at the back post, who tapped it in. *3–2!*

Wow, what drama! While the crowd went wild all around him, Kevin hugged his teammates and then urged them to keep calm and concentrate. It wasn't over yet; they still had fifteen minutes of defending to do. It was only when at last the final whistle blew that Kevin allowed himself to celebrate properly. City had done it; they had bounced back from 2–0 down to win the Premier League title!

Yesssssssssss!

In the biggest moment of the biggest game, Kevin had stepped up to become City's hero. Now, could he do the same for Belgium at the World Cup in Qatar?

DECLAN
RICE

PART 1

THE KID FROM KINGSTON WITH A WORLD CUP DREAM

During the summer of 2018, Declan had a huge and very difficult decision to make. So far, at international level, he had represented the Republic of Ireland, the country where his grandparents were from. He had proudly played for them at every age level, from Under-16 through to Under-21, and then in March, aged just nineteen, he had been selected to make his senior debut. Declan loved being one of 'The Boys in Green', and the manager, Martin O'Neill, had even described him as a future Ireland captain.

Wow, that sounded brilliant, but now following his big, break-out season at West Ham, suddenly there was also interest from England, the country where

Declan had been born and lived his whole life. The national team really needed a dynamic new defensive midfielder like him, and the England manager, Gareth Southgate, had even arranged a meeting to speak to him about changing countries.

Ireland or England? *Arggghhh* – Declan didn't know which to choose! As a kid growing up in Kingston upon Thames in south-west London and training at the Chelsea academy, his hero had been John Terry and he had supported England at every major tournament. There was still time for him to make the switch and play for the Three Lions instead, but Declan knew that if he did that, he would be disappointing a lot of Irish people, including O'Neill. In the end, he decided to take some time off to properly think things through.

That summer while Declan was making up his mind, the 2018 World Cup was taking place in Russia. England were one of the teams competing for the trophy – but unfortunately the Republic of Ireland hadn't qualified for the tournament since 2002, so Declan had only one team to support: England.

The Three Lions weren't expected to do that well, but with each excellent result:

The last-minute win against Tunisia...

The 6 −1 thrashing of Panama...

The penalty shoot-out victory over Colombia...

The quarter-final conquest of Sweden...

...World Cup fever spread further and further across the country. In parks, pubs, homes and streets all over England, fans were going wild, singing, 'Football's Coming Home!' As the buzz built and built, a thought was growing in Declan's mind:

'How cool would it be to play for England at a World Cup?!'

Declan was desperate to experience the excitement of playing in football's greatest competition, and with England, there was a good chance that dream might come true. His best friend, Mason Mount, already played for the Under-21s, and he was desperate for Declan to join him there.

'Come on – me and you could be in the England midfield at the next World Cup!'

That did sound amazing, but Declan refused to rush

and make his mind up straight away. Another seven months passed before he announced his final decision:

'...to submit a written request to Fifa for the transfer of my international registration from the Republic of Ireland to England...'

That was the first step; next, Declan had to work extra hard at West Ham to earn a place in Southgate's senior England squad. Luckily, that didn't take long at all. Just one month later, Declan was standing on the sidelines at Wembley Stadium, with Three Lions on his shirt, about to make his England debut against the Czech Republic.

Replacing Number 10 Dele Alli... Number 16 DECLAN RICE!

HURRRAAAAAAAAAYYYYYYYYYY!

Unbelievable! The crowd roared loudly, and Declan raced out onto the pitch, ready to start his road to the 2022 World Cup. Since the tournament in 2018, Southgate had switched the team's formation, from a 3-5-2 to a 4-3-3. That meant there was one extra spot up for grabs in the centre of midfield, and Declan was determined to make that his.

England were already winning the match 3–0, but there was still time for him to make an impact. His main job was to stay back and protect the defence, and that's what he did, winning the ball back for his team with clever tackles and interceptions.

With Declan sitting deep, England's other midfielders were free to push forward on the attack. Ross Barkley got the ball and ran with it, before setting up Raheem Sterling to complete his hat-trick. *4–0!*

Declan could do a lot more than just defend, though. In the eighty-third minute, he calmly collected the ball in his own half, looked up, and split the Czech midfield with a brilliant pass to Jadon Sancho. Jadon dribbled forward and slid it left to England's other debutant, Callum Hudson-Odoi. His shot was saved, but the rebound bounced in off a defender. *5–0!*

As a big grin spread across his face, Declan threw his arms up in the air. What a dream debut! Now, he just had to keep his great West Ham form going and keep his place in the England midfield.

Three days later, Declan played the full ninety

minutes as they thrashed Montenegro 5–1, and then in June, he played 106 minutes as England lost 2–1 in extra-time against the Netherlands in the UEFA Nations League semi-finals.

It was a disappointing defeat for the team, and also an important reminder for Declan that he still had lots to learn at the highest level. It had been his first real test playing against Frenkie de Jong and Gini Wijnaldum, two top midfielders who were so comfortable on the ball. On this occasion, he had lost the battle, but Declan didn't let it get him down for long. He was still young and new to international football, and the experience would help him to improve as a player.

Eighteen months later, when England took on Belgium, the top ranked team in the world, Declan did a much better job in the midfield battle against Kevin De Bruyne, Youri Tielemans and Axel Witsel. When Belgium took an early lead, Declan helped to keep England calm and organised as they came back to win. And who scored the winning goal? His best mate, Mason!

Yes, their dream of playing together in the England midfield had already come true and that next World Cup was now only two years away. First, however, the Three Lions would have to qualify for the tournament in Qatar.

PART 2

ENGLAND'S MAIN MAN IN MIDFIELD

31 March 2021, Wembley Stadium

'Let's goooo!' Declan clapped and cheered as
the England team walked out onto the pitch at
Wembley. With the stadium sadly still empty due
to the coronavirus pandemic, the players had to fire
themselves up for the big game ahead of them.

After two comfortable wins over San Marino and
Albania, the Three Lions were about to take on
the other top team in their World Cup qualification
group, Poland. Although their main superstar, Robert
Lewandowski, was out injured, they still had lots of
other talented players, like striker Krzysztof Piatek

and midfielder Piotr Zieliński, who both played for big clubs in Italy.

It certainly wasn't going to be an easy win for England, but Declan was looking forward to a tough midfield battle. On the opposite side, Grzegorz Krychowiak had seventy-eight international caps for Poland, which was more than Declan, Mason and Kalvin Phillips combined! Still, what they lacked in experience, England's new midfield three certainly made up for with energy, talent and drive.

Straight from the kick-off, they took control of the game, moving the ball around with calm composure. While Mason and Kalvin pushed forward whenever possible, Declan stayed in a much deeper position. He was always there if anyone wanted to pass to him, but protecting the defence was his number one priority.

For now, though, England were on the attack. In the eighteenth minute, Raheem used his speed to race into the box, where he was fouled by a Polish defender. *Penalty!*

Up stepped captain Harry Kane to score. *1–0!*

So far so good, but Declan wasn't getting carried away. This was an important match and Poland were a dangerous team, so he stayed focused and stayed back, alert to any signs of a potential counterattack.

He used his intelligence to make interceptions,

His timing to win tackles,

His strength to steal possession,

And his energy to always be in the right place at the right time for England.

Well done, Dec!

Then once he'd won the ball back, Declan dribbled it forward as far as he could and picked out a teammate with an accurate pass to launch another attack. He made that difficult defensive midfield role look so simple. At the age of twenty-two, it was amazing how comfortable he seemed at the centre of the England team already, as if it was his 115th cap, rather than only his fifteenth.

Early in the second half, however, disaster struck for England. John Stones gave the ball away in defence and Jakub Moder pounced to equalise for Poland, before Declan could sprint back and stop him. *1–1!*

Game on! But Declan didn't panic and push forward up the pitch; instead, he showed the discipline to hold his position and allow England's attackers to do what they did best: attack!

Raheem went on a weaving run through the Polish defence, until eventually the keeper stopped him. *BLOCK!*

Phil Foden won a free kick in a good area, but he failed to get his strike over the wall. MISS!

Mason set up Phil again, but his shot was too weak to really trouble the keeper. SAVE!

Oh dear, were England heading for a disappointing draw? No – fortunately, in the eighty-fourth minute, the winning goal arrived at last. From a corner-kick, John headed the ball down to Harry Maguire, who blasted a powerful shot past the keeper. *2–1!*

'Yesssssssss!' Declan roared, pumping his fists with passion and relief. Then he ran back for the restart, ready for ten more minutes of defending.

When the final whistle blew, Declan was so exhausted that he had to hobble over to hug Mason, but all that tireless ball-winning had been worth it. For England, it was a crucial win on the road to the 2022 World Cup, and a match that really confirmed their new main man in midfield.

'I thought Declan Rice's performances across all of the games has been excellent,' Southgate praised him at the press conference afterwards. 'His reading of danger, the number of recoveries he gets in front of that back four, but also he used the ball and drove forward with it really well.'

Just two years after making his England debut, Declan was now one of the first names on the manager's teamsheet. He had successfully climbed above Harry Winks, Eric Dier, Fabian Delph and even Liverpool captain Jordan Henderson to claim that starting spot in defensive midfield.

'3 wins out of 3 from the boys!' Declan posted on social media that night with a picture of him proudly holding the Player of the Match trophy. 'Let's keep pushing.'

With each victory, England were getting closer to the World Cup in Qatar, and they were also building up confidence ahead of their next exciting challenge – Euro 2020, which was taking place one year later than originally planned because of the COVID-19 pandemic.

PART 3

EURO HIGHS
AND LOWS

'Reaching the semi-finals at the 2018 World Cup was a huge step forward for us,' Southgate told his England players when they arrived at the team base camp ahead of Euro 2020. 'Take confidence from that, but we'll have to be even better to win this tournament.'

Challenge accepted! Declan couldn't wait. Being in the same England squad as Mason at a major tournament was already a childhood dream come true, but things got even better when Southgate announced the starting line-up for their first group game – they were in the same England midfield! Just like against Poland in the World Cup qualifiers,

Mason would be playing a little higher up the pitch, with Declan and Kalvin taking charge in front of the back four.

England's first Euro 2020 opponents were Croatia, the team that had beaten them in the World Cup semi-finals in 2018. Revenge would be sweet, but it wouldn't be easy. Their biggest threat would come from captain Luka Modric´, and Declan expected to spend a lot of the afternoon shadowing the Real Madrid star.

'If we shut him down, we take a big step towards shutting Croatia down' – that was Declan's plan and he executed it perfectly, helping England to bag a 1–0 win with a typical all-action performance. After that strong start, a disappointing 0–0 draw followed against Scotland, then a narrow victory over the Czech Republic. Things weren't quite clicking yet for England in attack, they were through to the Round of 16 and they still hadn't conceded a single goal.

Next up: Germany! Declan had been excited for all of the group games, but the build-up to a knockout game against England's greatest rivals at

Wembley was a whole new level of anticipation. 'The stakes will be high,' he said to Mason during one training session. 'If we win, we'll be heroes. If we lose, well... we probably shouldn't turn on the TV for a while.'

Declan was expecting a physical battle against the Germans, and that suited him just fine. 'Let's gooooooo!' he told himself as the players began the walk out onto the pitch.

It was physical and bruising, but he was never one to shy away from a tackle, even after picking up an early yellow card. He prowled around midfield, tracking runs and rushing in to break up attacks, but for almost seventy-five minutes, the match was a tense stalemate. Then Declan watched as Luke Shaw crossed from the left and Raheem steered a first-time shot into the net. 1–0!

'Come onnnnnnn!' As Wembley went wild, Declan punched the air and raced over to jump on the pile of celebrating teammates. These were the kinds of moments he had pictured as a kid – and now he was right in the middle of them! Harry Kane added a second goal right at the end to send England through to the quarter-finals.

There, they faced Ukraine, and for the first time in the tournament, Declan and his teammates would be leaving Wembley. 'We've just got to find a way to win in Rome,' he said to Mason as they waited for the flight to Italy. 'Then we get the semi-final and final back at Wembley.'

In fact, the quarter-final turned out to be England's easiest game of the tournament. Harry got them off to a dream start, with a sharp finish from Raheem's pass, and then they piled forward in search of some knockout blows. Declan's eyes lit up when the ball bounced invitingly in front of him, but his powerful shot was well saved by the Ukraine keeper. *Noooooooooooo* – so close to a first Euro goal!

After half-time, England quickly took charge, scoring two in five minutes. With the game wrapped up and Declan one yellow card away from suspension, Southgate decided to take him off and give him a well-deserved rest. England were definitely going to need Declan for their big Euro semi-final against Denmark.

There was a slightly nervous atmosphere at Wembley as the teams walked out for the anthems – and it only got tenser when Denmark took the lead with a stunning free kick. Uh-oh – how would England respond? It was the first goal they had conceded at the tournament, but Declan knew there was plenty of time to hit back. He just settled himself down and focused on playing the simple pass.

Nine minutes later, England got their equaliser, but there was nothing to separate the teams in the second half. The semi-final headed into extra time, and Declan was soon watching with the rest of the players and coaches from the bench as Southgate went with fresh legs in midfield.

Come on, England!

Just when Declan began to worry it might go all the way to a shoot-out, Raheem danced his way into the penalty area and fell as a Denmark defender closed in on him. 'Penalty!' Declan screamed along with tens of thousands of fans around him. The referee pointed to the spot and Harry sent England into the final, firing in the rebound after his penalty was saved. *2–1!*

When the final whistle blew, Declan jogged onto the pitch to celebrate with his terrific teammates. It was a night they would all remember. They were achieving amazing things together – they would be playing in the Euro 2020 final!

After all the hugging, dancing, singing and high-fiving, the England players turned their focus to the final against Italy. This would be their toughest game of the tournament, but they felt ready for it.

If Declan thought Wembley was rocking in the semi-final, it was even louder as the players walked out for the final. England were back in a major men's final for the first time in fifty-five years and a buzz of expectation filled the stadium.

Declan belted out the national anthem with his teammates and then steadied himself. It was normal to have nerves for this kind of game and he just wanted to channel them into an energetic, ball-winning performance that the nation needed from him.

With a packed crowd cheering them on, England

got off to a dream start. From a quick attack down the right, a deep cross reached Luke shaw at the back post, and he smashed a first-time shot off the post and into the back of the net. *1–0!*

Up in the stands, the fans went crazy, but down on the pitch, Declan wasn't getting carried away. He kept on winning his battles, accepting the challenge of rattling an Italy midfield that had been dominant throughout the tournament. He pounced on every loose ball and cut off the passing angles between the lines.

Well done, Dec!

In the second half, however, Italy clawed their way back into the game. Even as he scurried around to close down space, Declan could feel England dropping deeper and deeper. The Italians made it 1–1 and then kept pushing for a second, winning goal.

With fifteen minutes to go, Southgate decided that it was time to make a change in midfield. Declan's heart sank when he saw his number on the assistant referee's electronic board, but he high-fived Jordan Henderson and then his manager as he left the pitch.

He just wished he could have stayed on and given even more for his team.

In the end, the Euro 2020 final went all the way to... PENALTIES! Declan's stomach was performing somersaults and his legs felt shaky as he walked around the huddle of England players guzzling water and preparing for penalties. He wasn't sure what to say and didn't want to affect their focus, so he just patted a few of the penalty takers on the back.

England started well, scoring their first two spot-kicks, but after that, everything started to go wrong. First Marcus Rashford hit the post, then Jadon Sancho's shot was saved. Jordan Pickford gave them a glimmer of hope by stopping Jorginho's penalty, but sadly Bukayo Saka couldn't score either. It was all over, and Italy were the new Champions of Europe, not England.

To get so close to glory was heartbreaking. Declan was devastated, but with tears in his eyes, he rushed over to support his brave teammates who had missed their penalties. They won together and they lost together – that was the new England way.

'Lads, I know it's painful right now, but I'm incredibly proud of what you've achieved,' Southgate said once his disappointed players were all back in the dressing room. 'We went toe-to-toe with the best teams in Europe and we're going to keep improving. The World Cup is only eighteen months away, and the rest of the world knows that we mean business now.'

PART 4

QATAR BOUND

Declan took a few weeks off to relax and recover after his England experience, but soon he was back out on the football pitch where he belonged. When the new 2021–22 season started, some players suffered a post-Euro 2020 slump, but not Declan; no, he seemed to be improving with every game. Not only was he doing his defensive midfield work, winning the ball back again and again with tackles and interceptions, but also, when the time was right, he was showing what he could do on the attack.

In the Premier League, Declan carried the ball forward with pace and power, played a one-two with Aaron Cresswell, and then fired a cross in towards

Michail Antonio. *West Ham 3, Leicester City 1!*

And in the Europa League, Declan did something even more special. Intercepting a pass in his own half, he raced forward up the left wing, leaving one defender stumbling behind him. As he looked up, he couldn't see any teammates in support, so Declan kept going himself, all the way into the box, where he trusted his left foot to drill in a low shot from a tight angle. It was perfectly placed, zipping through the goalkeeper's legs and into the net. *Dinamo Zagreb 0, West Ham 2!*

What a sensational solo goal! Declan stood there in front of the West Ham fans with his arms out wide, enjoying his latest hero moment.

In England's next World Cup qualifier against Hungary, Declan spent most of the game in a deep position, protecting the defence. But in the eighty-fifth minute, with his team winning 3–0, he decided it was time to move further up the pitch. When the ball came to him, he curled a beautiful pass out to Jack Grealish on the right wing, who cut inside and then laid it back to him. Declan's first-time strike flew through the crowded penalty area and squirmed under the keeper.

Goooooooooooooooooooaaaaaaaaaaaaaaaaaallllllllllllll lllllllllll!!!!!!!!!!!!!!!!!!

'Yesssssssss!' Declan yelled out with a huge smile on his face as Kalvin raced over to celebrate with him. Stops and shots – he was becoming the complete midfield player, for both club and country.

With such a busy international schedule, Southgate decided to rest Declan for the 4–0 win over Andorra. For England's big match away against Poland, however, he was back at the heart of the midfield, fighting hard for every ball. The Three Lions were on track to make it six wins out of six, thanks to a wondergoal from Harry Kane, until the ninety-second minute, when England lost their concentration and allowed Poland to equalise. *1–1!*

Noooooooooo! Declan couldn't believe it – all that hard work gone to waste! Oh well, never mind, England were still one point closer to qualifying for Qatar, and they were still four points clear at the top of Group I with four games to go...

Andorra 0 England 5:

Declan didn't play in the match, but he was there on the bench, cheering his team to a comfortable victory.

England 1 Hungary 1:

It wasn't the win they were looking for, but it wasn't the worst result either, especially after going 1–0 down. The most important thing was that England were still three points clear of Poland in first place, with two final games to go...

Albania at home, followed by San Marino away – on paper, picking up four more points sounded like a fairly simple task, but the England players weren't leaving anything to chance. They were determined to get the job done properly, and they wouldn't relax until World Cup qualification was 100 per cent secured.

Declan arrived at St George's Park with the rest of the squad, but sadly he was unable to train due to illness. He was hoping to be feeling better in time for the first match against Albania, but no, in the end he had to withdraw and return to West Ham. His

England teammates would just have to complete the last part of the road to the World Cup without him.

'Gutted to be missing the game tonight!' Declan wrote on social media. 'Wishing all the boys the best of luck. Come on England.'

Fortunately, it turned out to be a match where they didn't really need their best defensive midfielder on the field. In front of a full crowd at Wembley, England were 5–0 up by half-time!

Harry Maguire headed in the first,

Harry Kane headed in the second,

Declan's replacement, Jordan Henderson, fired in the third…

…and then Harry Kane added two more to complete another England hat-trick.

'Great win boys!' Declan tweeted after the game. 'One step closer to where we want to be.'

In fact, they were now just one point away from World Cup qualification. Surely, England weren't going to slip up against their last opponents, San Marino, the 210th-ranked national team in the world?

No, the Three Lions doubled their 5–0 win over

Albania by thrashing San Marino 10–0.

'Man, I wish we were playing in this game,' Declan messaged Mason, who was missing the match through injury. 'We could have had a hat-trick each!'

'Me yeah, but you?' his friend replied cheekily. 'You've never scored a hat-trick in your life, bro!'

At the final whistle, Declan punched the air and posted a message to his fans:

'10/10. Qatar bound.'

England had reached the World Cup semi-finals in 2018, the Euros final in 2021, so how far would they go in 2022? Could they go all the way and win their first major tournament since 1966? Declan couldn't wait to play his part and make his country proud. For the kid from Kingston, his World Cup dream was about to come true.

LIONEL
MESSI

PART 1

2018: ANOTHER WORLD CUP, THE SAME SAD STORY

30 June 2018, Ak Bars Arena, Russia

The pressure was on and the noise was deafening, but Lionel still looked calm and relaxed as he led the players out onto the pitch.

'Good to see you, mate,' he said with a smile as he shared a hug with Samuel Umtiti, 'and good luck today!'

Most of the time, Lionel and Samuel were club teammates at Barcelona, but not in this match. Today, they were international rivals because Argentina were taking on France in the World Cup Round of 16.

Vamos, Vamos Argentina!

Messi! Messi! Messi!

Twelve years on from his first appearance at the
tournament, Lionel was still yet to win the World Cup
with Argentina. 'La Albiceleste' had come so close in
2014, but in the final against Germany, they had lost
in extra-time. Could they go one better and lift the
trophy this time in 2018? That was the aim. Lionel
was desperate to follow in the footsteps of Argentina's
other great football genius, Diego Maradona, and
collect the one major winners' medal he was missing.
If he succeeded, he would surely be the 'GOAT', the
greatest of all time.

So far at the tournament, however, Argentina hadn't
looked like future World Champions at all. They
looked weak and slow at the back, and despite a front
three of Lionel, Ángel Di María, and Sergio Agüero,
they were also struggling to score goals in attack.
After a disappointing opening draw with Iceland, *La
Albiceleste* had then suffered a shock 3–0 defeat to
Croatia.

Oh dear, were they going out in the group stage?
No, thanks to a lovely goal from Lionel and a late

volley from Marcos Rojo, Argentina had beaten Nigeria 2–1 and scraped their way through to the World Cup Round of 16. There, they now faced France, one of the tournament favourites.

As well as experienced players like Raphaël Varane, Paul Pogba, and Antoine Griezmann, France also had football's most exciting young superstar, Kylian Mbappé. With his incredible speed and skill, he would be a very dangerous opponent for Argentina's dodgy defence...

In the twelfth minute, Mbappé got the ball in his own half and ZOOM! he set off on a sensational run, dribbling past Éver Banega...

Then Nicolás Tagliafico...

And then Javier Mascherano too.

The only defender left was Marcos, and all he could do to stop Mbappé was pull him to the floor. Penalty – *1–0 to France!*

Uh-oh, Argentina were losing already, but with world-class players like Lionel on the pitch, they always believed they had a chance of winning.

Ángel equalised before half-time with a stunning

strike, and then just after the break, Lionel turned on the edge of the box and curled the ball goalwards. His shot flicked off Gabriel Mercado's boot and flew past Hugo Lloris.

'Yesssssssssss!' Lionel yelled as he jumped into Gabriel's arms. From 1–0 down, they were now winning 2–1!

Unfortunately, however, Argentina couldn't hold on to that lead for long. In the space of eleven mad minutes, France's right-back Benjamin Pavard scored a glorious goal, and then Mbappé added two more of his own. *4–2 to France!*

'Noooooooooo!' As he watched the ball roll into the Argentina net for the fourth time, Lionel let his head drop into his hand. What were the defenders doing?! They were competing at a World Cup – where was the organisation, the communication, the fighting spirit? They were being completely outpaced and outplayed by France's attackers.

There were still twenty-five minutes to go, but was there any way back for Argentina? Lionel did his best to create some magic for his team. With a flick of his left foot and a burst of speed, he dribbled between three defenders and into the box, but as he went to shoot, he slipped, sending the ball trickling straight towards the keeper.

'Arghhhhhh!' Lionel screamed out in frustration, before picking himself up and playing on. Argentina's World Cup wasn't over yet.

Deep in injury time, Lionel looked up and chipped a beautiful cross to the back post, where Sergio headed the ball down into the bottom corner. *4–3!*

'Vamooooooooos!' Lionel roared out to his teammates as they raced back for the restart, but sadly, there wasn't enough time to score again. Seconds later, the final whistle blew, and Argentina's 2018 World Cup was officially over.

After shaking hands with his opponents, Lionel stood alone on the pitch for ages with his hands on his hips and a sad, thoughtful look on his face. Was that it, his last chance to win a major international trophy gone? And with Mbappé emerging as world football's new superstar, did that make Lionel a superstar of the past?

'No way,' he decided with fierce determination, 'I'm still only thirty-one years old; I'm not ready to give up on my goal yet. Bring on the next big competition!'

PART 2

PROGRESS AND PAIN

The next big competition for Argentina was the 2019 Copa América. By the time the tournament began in Brazil, a year had passed since their World Cup disappointment, and a lot had changed for *La Albiceleste*. The national team had a new manager, Lionel Scaloni, and lots of new players too, including:

Defender Germán Pezzella,

Midfielders Rodrigo De Paul and Leandro Paredes,

And attacker Lautaro Martínez.

It wasn't a totally new team, though. Many of Argentina's most experienced stars were still there: Nicolás Otamendi, Ángel, Sergio, and of course their leader and number one superstar, Lionel. He couldn't wait to play at the Copa América again, and hopefully, lift the trophy at last for his country. Would he be fifth time lucky at the tournament?

After a terrible start against Colombia, Argentina got better and better as the competition went on:

A draw with Paraguay,

Then a win over Qatar to finish second in the group,

Then another victory against Venezuela in the quarter-finals.

'Come on, we can win this!' Lionel cried out as the players celebrated together. At last, Argentina were starting to look like a well-organised team again – strong at the back and dangerous in attack. Their next game, however, was going to be a serious test of their progress. Were they good enough to beat the hosts, Brazil?

The Copa América semi-final was a fierce contest right from the start, with tackles flying in everywhere. In the twentieth minute, Brazil took the lead through Gabriel Jesus, but Argentina didn't back down. With Lionel leading the way, they kept pushing forward on the attack, searching for an equaliser...

Sergio's header hit the crossbar,

Lautaro's shot flew straight at Alisson,

And then Lionel's swerving strike smacked against the post.

Nooooooooooooooo!

If they carried on attacking so brilliantly, surely Argentina would score eventually? In the seventieth minute, Lautaro passed the ball to Lionel, who looked to feed it through to Sergio on the run. By the time the ball arrived, however, Sergio was lying on the ground in the box, after being tripped by Dani Alves.

'Penalty!' all the Argentina players and supporters called out, but the referee shook his head. 'Play on!' he shouted, and seconds later, Brazil went up the other end and scored a second goal on the counterattack.

'No way, we should have had a penalty – check with VAR!' Lionel and his teammates were furious – it was so unfair! Fifteen minutes later, they called for another penalty after a bad foul on Nicolás, but again, the referee said no.

At the final whistle, Lionel stood there with his

hands on his hips again, but this time, the look on his face wasn't sad and thoughtful; it was annoyed and frustrated. Because Argentina really didn't deserve to be knocked out of the Copa América like that; they had been as good as Brazil, if not better, but it felt like all of the big decisions had gone against them.

'The referee was on their side,' Lionel told the media afterwards, before his anger eventually began to fade.

What was done was done, and plus, Argentina still had one more game to go: a third-place play-off against Chile. No, it wasn't the Copa América final, but it was still a match that they really wanted to win.

From deep in his own half, Lionel dribbled the ball forward, skipping away from one tackle, then another, until eventually the third sent him tumbling to the floor. Free kick!

As soon as he was back on his feet, Lionel looked up and spotted Sergio on the move. Excellent! With a clever, quick free kick, he caught Chile by surprise. His pass was perfect – right between the two centre-backs and into the path of Sergio, who rounded the keeper and fired into the empty net. 1–0 to Argentina!

'Come onnnnnn!' Sergio shouted, pointing over at his good friend, Lionel. What a deadly duo they were, but the new Argentina were much more than a two-man team. Ten minutes later, Paulo Dybala made it 2–0 with a classy chip over the diving keeper.

As *La Albiceleste* cruised to victory, Chile got more and more aggressive with their fouling. Lionel managed to keep his cool through all the kicks and shirt pulls, but with half-time approaching, his match came to a very abrupt end. After battling for the ball by the touchline, the Chile centre-back Gary Medel turned angrily and squared up to Lionel, pushing his head towards his face.

'Woah, what are you doing?' Lionel cried out in shock, and he was about to get an even bigger surprise. Because when the referee raced over, waving a red card in the air, he showed one to Medel, and then one to him too!

'No way – I'm innocent!' Lionel tried his best to explain, but it was no use. His tournament was over, and with a shake of the head, he trudged off down the tunnel.

Oh well, at the end of a difficult and dramatic Copa América, at least Lionel could look forward with positivity. His team's progress was way more important than the pain of some bad penalty decisions and a ridiculous red card. The new Argentina was developing nicely, and Lionel was determined to lead them to tournament victory eventually...

PART 3

COPA AMÉRICA CHAMPIONS AT LAST!

The next Copa América was delayed due to COVID-19, but it finally took place in Brazil in June 2021. By then, Scaloni had strengthened his squad even further, especially in defence. Now, Argentina had:

A new goalkeeper: Emi Martínez,

A new centre-back: Cristian Romero,

Two new right-backs: Nahuel Molina and Gonzalo Montiel,

And an extra defensive midfielder: Guido Rodríguez. Much better!

'Come on, we can win this!' Lionel cried out as he led his Argentina teammates out for their first game against Chile. Although it felt weird walking out into an empty stadium due to the coronavirus pandemic, he still felt the same old buzz about playing for his country at the Copa América. So, would it be sixth time lucky for Lionel in the competition?

From the moment the tournament started, it was clear that Argentina's captain was in fine form and more determined than ever to achieve his Copa América dream. In the thirty-third minute against Chile, he coolly curled a free kick into the top-right corner, as if it was the easiest thing in the world. *1–0!*

Goooooooooooooooooooooooaaaaaaaaaaaaaaaaallllllllllllllll llllllllllllll!!!!!!!!!!!!!!!!!!!!

'Vamoooooooooooos!' Lionel shouted with passion as he jumped up and punched the air. This was going to be Argentina's year; he could feel it already. After setting up the winner against Uruguay with an incredible cross to Guido, he grabbed two goals and an assist in a 4–1 thrashing of Bolivia.

So far so good, but as Lionel knew well, the most difficult matches were still to come in the knockout stage.

First up, in the quarter-finals, Argentina faced Ecuador. It took forty minutes of trying, but eventually Lionel found a way through their strong defence. With a first-time flick of his left foot, he set up Rodrigo for a simple finish. *1–0!*

'Thanks Leo, you're the best!' Rodrigo cried out as he jumped into his captain's arms.

Late in the second half, Lionel unselfishly poked the ball across to Lautaro for goal number two, and then to put the cherry on the cake, he stepped up and scored his second free kick of the tournament in the final seconds.

Goooooooooooooooooooooaaaaaaaaaaaaaaaaaalllllllllllllll llllllllllll!!!!!!!!!!!!!!!!!!!

Hurray, Argentina were through to the Copa América semi-finals again! Now, could they stay calm and beat Colombia to reach the final? Their chances looked good in the seventh minute, when Lionel turned in the box and laid the ball back to Lautaro, who swept it into the bottom corner. *1–0!*

'Man, I love playing with you!' Argentina's goalscorer shouted as he carried Lionel on his back over to the fans.

What a start! There was still a lot of football left, though, and in the second half, Colombia came back and equalised. Game on – so, which team would score the winning goal? The answer was... neither. The best chance fell to Lionel, but his shot smacked off the post and Rodrigo's rebound was blocked. Moments later, the final whistle blew, and the semi-final went straight to... A PENALTY SHOOT-OUT!

'Hey, you've got this, Leo,' his teammate Papu Gómez assured him as the Argentina players huddled together on the pitch.

Lionel had missed his spot-kick in the 2016 Copa América final, but despite the bad memories, he went first for his country as usual. This was his chance to put things right. After a short run-up, he calmly fired an unstoppable shot into the top corner. *GOAL!*

After a quick fist-pump, Lionel walked over to wish his keeper luck. Seven penalties later, Emi was the hero with three super saves, and Argentina were into the final!

Hurrraaaaayyyyyyyyyy!

'So proud and happy to be part of this group,' Lionel posted on social media as he prepared for what would be his fourth Copa América final. He had finished on the losing team in 2007, 2015 and 2016, but this time would be different. He had never felt more motivated to win a football match, especially as their opponents in the final would be their big rivals Brazil, who had beaten them in the semi-finals two years before.

Vamos, vamos Argentina!

Despite the pressure and excitement, however, Lionel looked totally calm as he led the Argentina team out onto the pitch for the final. Yes, he was their superstar, captain, and top scorer with four goals in the tournament, but to lift the Copa América trophy at last, they would all have to work together. That was the secret to the new Argentina side – rather than just a group of talented individuals, they were a strong, united team.

With the Brazil defenders double-marking Lionel, it was Ángel who turned out to be Argentina's matchwinner. In the twenty-second minute, he collected a beautiful long pass from Rodrigo and then lobbed the ball over Ederson and into the net. *1–0!*

'Yesssssss!' Lionel yelled out joyfully, while racing over to celebrate with Ángel. But really, they were all heroes. Every single Argentinian played their part in the victory, from Emi making saves in goal all the way through to Lautaro making runs up front. The win was one big squad effort.

This time, at the final whistle, Lionel wasn't left standing alone on the halfway line. No, as he collapsed to his knees and cried, he was surrounded by tearful teammates.

'Leo, we did it, we did it!'

What an amazing and emotional moment – after sixteen years as an Argentina international, Lionel had finally won his first major tournament! After lots of hugs and smiles, the players lifted their leader up and tossed him high into the air again and again.

Hurray! Hurray! Hurray!

Then, for the greatest moment of all: trophy time! Captain Lionel carried it carefully over to his teammates and then, holding it above his head, he bounced up and down with delight. He had been waiting so long to taste success with Argentina.

Campeones, Campeones, Olé! Olé! Olé!

What a night and what a team! Lionel loved every single one of them – from his old friends Sergio, Ángel and Nicolás to the new stars like Emi, Rodrigo and Lautaro. Together, they had launched an exciting new era for Argentina and the next World Cup was less than eighteen months away.

PART 4

SEE YOU
IN QATAR!

Before they could start looking ahead to the 2022
World Cup in Qatar, however, Argentina had to make
sure that they qualified. With six games played, they
still hadn't lost a single one, but now, *La Albiceleste*
needed to finish what they had started.

'Vamoooooooos!' Lionel urged his teammates on.
Still buzzing from their Copa América triumph, they
carried on where they had left off at the tournament.
Lautaro was the star of the show when Argentina won
3–1 against Venezuela, and then Lionel led the way
when they beat Bolivia.

First, he nutmegged his way past his marker and
curled a shot into the far corner from the edge of the

penalty area. *1–0!*

*Goooooooooooooooooooaaaaaaaaaaaaaaaaaallllllllllllll
llllllllllll!!!!!!!!!!!!!!!!!!!!*

Racing away to celebrate, Lionel kissed the
Argentina badge on his shirt. He really did love playing
for his country. Later on, he danced his way through
the box, playing a double one-two with Lautaro,
before chipping the ball past the keeper. *2–0!*

Wow, what a beautiful bit of football! Then, as a
finale, Lionel tapped in from close range to grab his
third goal of the game. *3–0!*

Hurray, for the seventh time in his career, Lionel
was an Argentina hat-trick hero! And that wasn't all;
he had also just overtaken Pelé as the top international
goalscorer in South American football history!

The most important thing, though, was that
Argentina had won again. They were now unbeaten
in twenty-two matches, and they were moving closer
and closer to World Cup qualification:

Paraguay 0 Argentina 0,
Argentina 3 Uruguay 0...

Again, it was Lionel who gave his team the lead,

although it was supposed to be a pass, not a shot. But after flying just past Nicolás González's outstretched boot, the ball flew past the Uruguay keeper too, and into the net. *1–0!*

Oh well, they all counted, and the Argentina players celebrated the goal as wildly as any other. Looking up at the roaring crowd, Lionel raised both arms above his head and pumped his fists with passion, as if to say, 'World Cup, here we come!'

...Argentina 1 Peru 0,

Uruguay 0 Argentina 1...

Another victory and another cleansheet – Argentina's united team of warriors were so nearly there now! One more point was all they needed...

...Argentina 0 Brazil 0.

Job done, goal achieved – *La Albiceleste* had qualified for the 2022 World Cup without a single defeat, and with four games to spare! Lionel had a message to send to all the amazing Argentina supporters:

'See you in Qatar!'

They only had twelve more months to wait until

the big event began. In the meantime, Lionel focused on starring for his new club PSG, alongside Neymar Jr, Kylian Mbappé and his old friend Ángel in attack. What a front four! Unfortunately, they couldn't win the Champions League together, but Lionel did lift his first French league title, as well as something very, very special: his seventh Ballon d'Or.

Surely, now he was officially the 'GOAT', whether he managed to win the World Cup or not? But for Lionel, football wasn't about individuals. So, in his speech at the awards ceremony in Paris, he made sure to thank all of his teammates, both for club and country.

At the end of his first season in France, Lionel met up with the Argentina squad again for two final international matches before a summer break. It was great to be back amongst his national team friends, but it wasn't all fun and laughs. With the World Cup coming soon, the squad had practice to do, preparations to make, and also another trophy to try and win: the CONMEBOL-UEFA Cup of Champions.

In the match people were calling 'the Finalissima',

it was Argentina versus Italy, the winners of the Copa
América versus the winners of Euro 2020. So, who
would be victorious – South America or Europe?

Everyone was expecting a tight game at Wembley
Stadium, but instead, Argentina cruised to a
comfortable victory. In the first twenty-five minutes,
they had defending to do, but after that, their
attackers came alive.

Lionel used his strength and skill to turn and escape
past Giovanni Di Lorenzo, before crossing the ball to
Lautaro for a tap-in. *1–0!*

'Come onnnnnnn!' Argentina's striker cried out as
he leapt into Lionel's open arms.

Then just before half-time, Lautaro burst forward
from the halfway line and slipped a brilliant ball
through to Ángel. *2–0!*

Argentina's forwards were on fire, and so were their
defenders. There was no way Nicolás and Cristian
were going to let Italy back into the game. *BLOCK!
HEADER! TACKLE!*

Vamooooooooooos!

Lionel was looking dangerous every time he

touched the ball, but he was desperate to grab a goal of his own. In the end, however, he had to settle for a second assist of the game. With only seconds to go, he dribbled at the Italian defence one last time, and then passed to Paulo, who finished in style. *3–0!*

Argentina were the Finalissima winners! As they celebrated on the pitch before collecting the trophy, the players lifted Lionel up and tossed him high into the air again and again, just like they had done after the Copa América final.

Hurray! Hurray! Hurray!

They were so lucky to have such a wonderful leader. Four days later, Argentina thrashed Estonia 5–0 in a friendly match, and how many of the goals did their captain score? All five!

Unbelievable! At the age of thirty-four, Lionel was hitting top form for his country. He was counting down the days until the World Cup in Qatar began.

CRISTIANO RONALDO

PART 1

MORE BIG GAMES, MORE BIG GOALS AND GLORY

It was 10 July 2016, and the Euros final of France vs Portugal was a match that Cristiano would never forget, for as long as he lived. That night, in Paris, he had experienced every emòtion. First, he had cried tears of sorrow as he hobbled off with an early injury, and then, ninety long minutes later, tears of pure joy as he lifted his first major international trophy at last, after nearly thirteen years of trying. Hurray, Portugal were the new European Champions!

After such an amazing achievement, some footballers might have just sat back and enjoyed the proud moment, thinking, 'Ahhhhh, job done!' But not Cristiano – no, that wasn't his style at all. He

was a superstar who was never satisfied; he always
wanted more. More big games, more big goals, and
most importantly of all, more glory. Now that Portugal
were the Champions of Europe, the next step was
becoming Champions of the World too!

With that ambition on his mind, Cristiano started
the 2018 World Cup in style. In Portugal's opening
group game, he scored his first goal in the fourth
minute and his second just before half-time. In the
second half, however, Spain fought back with two
quick goals to take a 3–2 lead. Oh dear, Portugal were
heading for a disappointing first defeat. Unless, their
incredible captain could somehow save the day...

In the eighty-eighth minute, Cristiano won a free
kick just outside the Spain penalty area, and of course,
he got up and grabbed the ball himself. There was no
way he was going to let any of his teammates take
it. After a few long, deep breaths, he looked up at
the target with fire in his eyes. This was it: his last
big chance to score an equaliser. When the referee's
whistle blew, Cristiano took a few short steps forward
and then curled the ball up over the wall and into the

top corner. His strike was so powerful and accurate that the keeper, David de Gea, didn't even move. *3–3!*

Goooooooooooooooooooooaaaaaaaaaaaaaaaaalllllllllllllll llllllllllll!!!!!!!!!!!!!!!!!!!!!

'What a genius!' the TV commentators cried as Cristiano raced away to celebrate with a 'Siuuuu!' in front of the fans. He had saved the day for his country yet again, with another big goal in another big game. And not only had he just become Portugal's World Cup hero, but he was also now a World Cup hat-trick hero too!

In the next match, Cristiano scored again, this time a determined diving header to beat Morocco. He wasn't going to be able to win the World Cup on his own, though. He needed more help from the young attackers around him. Gonçalo Guedes, André Silva, João Mário, Bernardo Silva, Bruno Fernandes – they were all talented players, so why weren't they showing it? Portugal couldn't rely on their captain to do it all.

When Cristiano missed a penalty against Iran in their final group game, they drew 1–1.

And when he failed to score against Uruguay in the Round of 16, they lost 2–1 and were knocked out.

Nooooo, not again! 2006, 2010, 2014 and now 2018 – another World Cup had ended in frustration for Cristiano. With an angry scowl on his face, he trudged off the pitch and straight down the tunnel.

So, at the age of thirty-three, was it time for him to give up on his World Cup-winning dream? After the tournament, Cristiano decided to take a break from international football and focus on his new club, Juventus. It wasn't long, however, before he was back playing for his country again. Why stop? As long as he kept looking after his body and avoided any serious injuries, there was no reason why Cristiano couldn't make it to the 2022 tournament in Qatar. And before that, there were other trophies for Portugal to try and win, starting with the new UEFA Nations League.

Although Cristiano hadn't played in any of the group games, the manager Fernando Santos put him straight into the squad for the finals, and then straight into the starting line-up for the semi-final against Switzerland. That turned out to be a very wise decision indeed.

In the twenty-fifth minute, Cristiano stepped up and fired a swerving free kick past the wall and into the bottom corner. *1–0!*

SIUUUU!

What a way to announce his return to international football! With a big smile on his face, Cristiano threw his arms out wide to hug all of his teammates.

'I'm BACK!'

Portugal weren't through to the Nations League final yet, though. In the second half, Switzerland equalised, and with five minutes left, it looked like the game was going to extra-time. Unless, someone could somehow save the day...

With time running out, Bernardo controlled the ball on the right wing and pulled it back to the edge of the penalty area, where he knew his captain was waiting. Cristiano reacted in a flash and rocketed a first-time shot past the keeper. *2–1!*

SIUUUU!

What a superstar he was – Cristiano had saved the day for Portugal yet again, with another big goal in another big game! Two minutes later, he dribbled into the Switzerland box, fooled the defender with two stepovers, and then guided a shot into the bottom corner. *3–1!*

SIUUUU!

Game over, Cristiano was a hat-trick hero once again, and he had helped Portugal to reach the Nations League final!

There, they faced the Netherlands in front of a loud home crowd at the Estádio do Dragão in Porto. With Virgil van Dijk and Matthijs de Ligt, the Dutch defence was very strong, but Cristiano was determined to make life difficult for them. He wasn't trying to do it all on his own anymore, though, because Portugal's talented young players were really starting to shine.

This time, when Cristiano didn't score, his team still managed to win. In the sixtieth minute, Bernardo dribbled his way brilliantly into the box, before cutting the ball back for Gonçalo to strike. *1–0!*

'Come onnnnn!' Cristiano cheered, high-fiving Bruno as they chased over to the corner to celebrate with Gonçalo and Bernardo.

Now, Portugal just had to stay strong and hold on for victory. Thirty minutes later, when the final whistle blew, Cristiano threw both arms high into the air and then raced over to his teammates. They had done it; together, they had won the Nations League!

After lots of hugs and high-fives, it was finally time for Cristiano to do his captain's job and collect the stylish silver trophy. When he picked it up, he gave it a quick kiss and then carried it over to the stage, where the other Portugal players were waiting impatiently.

Oooooooohhhhhhhhhhhhhh...

With a cheeky smile on his face, Cristiano let the tension build for a bit, before eventually lifting the trophy high into the Porto sky.

...Hurrrraaaaaaaaaaaaaaayyyyy!

PART 2

GOALS GALORE AT EURO 2020

First, there had been Euro 2016, then the 2018–19 UEFA Nations League... but now could Cristiano complete an international trophy hat-trick by leading Portugal to glory at Euro 2020?

As ever, he was full of belief and desire. 'I feel as motivated or even more motivated than in 2004 when I played my first European tournament,' Cristiano told the media.

Defending that Euro title was going to be a very difficult task, however. Portugal would have to play really well to even get out of Group F, the tournament's 'Group of Death', where they faced Hungary and then the last two World Cup champions,

France and Germany.

It was a challenging start, but with Cristiano on the pitch, anything felt possible for Portugal. Plus Bruno and Bernardo, of course! One thing was for sure, though: they simply had to win their opening game against Hungary. Otherwise, it could be tournament over straight away.

At the Puskás Aréna in Budapest, Portugal had most of the possession and created lots of chances, but they couldn't seem to score. Diogo Jota had several strikes saved, and then Cristiano somehow flicked Bruno's cross over the bar, despite being inside the six-yard box.

'Nooooooo!' Cristiano cried out, with his head in his hands. How on earth had he missed such an easy chance? The supporters were just as shocked as he was.

As the second half ticked by, the Portugal players took more and more shots, but still they couldn't beat the Hungary keeper. Oh dear, was the game going to end in a disappointing draw? No, with less than ten minutes to go, they finally got the crucial goal they needed, and this time, it wasn't Cristiano who scored it. Instead, it was the left-back, Raphaël Guerreiro. 1–0 at last!

After that breakthrough, Cristiano added two more late goals to seal the victory for Portugal. First, he fired in a penalty, and then he played a double one-two with Rafa Silva, before dribbling around the goalkeeper. *3–0!*

Gooooooooooooooooooooaaaaaaaaaaaaaaaaallllllllllllllll llllllllllllll!!!!!!!!!!!!!!!!!!!!

SIUUUU!

Cristiano was all smiles now – not only were his team off to a winning start, but he was also the new record goalscorer in men's European Championship history!

'Força Portugal!' he tweeted after the match.

Right, could they now go on and beat Germany too? Cristiano got them off to the perfect start with a tap-in after fifteen minutes, but from 1–0 up, Portugal fell to a 4–2 defeat, thanks to two own goals and some disastrous defending.

As he trudged off the pitch, Cristiano sighed

and shook his head in dismay, but at least their tournament wasn't over yet. With a win or a draw against France, they could still reach the Round of 16...

It turned out to be the Cristiano vs Karim Benzema Show. For years, they had been teammates at Real Madrid, but now they were international rivals, battling to be the matchwinner.

In the first half, Cristiano scored from the penalty spot. 1–0!

Then so did Karim. *1–1!*

In the second half, Karim scored again. *2–1!*

Then so did Cristiano. *2–2!*

And that's how it finished. Thanks to another heroic performance from their captain, Portugal had picked up the one point they needed to make it through as one of the best third-placed teams. Hurray! After the final whistle, Cristiano walked around the field hugging his teammates and blowing kisses to the fans. It was job done... for now.

Next up in the knockout stages, Portugal would face Belgium, the top-ranked team in the world. But with Cristiano on the pitch, anything felt possible.

'Let's go!' he posted on social media, alongside a photo of him on the plane to Spain with his long-time teammate Pepe. Hopefully, their big-game experience would help get them through to the quarter-finals.

When the match kicked off, it was Portugal who created the first goalscoring chances. Diogo scuffed a shot wide and then Thibaut Courtois had to dive down low to stop a ferocious free kick from Cristiano.

'Ooooohhhhhhhhhhhhhhh!' groaned the supporters in the stadium. They were so used to seeing their leader score from positions like that. 'Unlucky, keep going!'

But unfortunately, it was Belgium who took the lead just before half-time, as Thorgan Hazard fired a swerving shot past Rui Patrício.

'Come onnn!' Cristiano cried out, throwing his arms up in anger. Why hadn't someone closed Hazard down quicker? Why hadn't the keeper done his job and saved his strike? Oh well, there was nothing they could do about it now; Portugal would just have to fight back and find a way to score themselves in the second half...

Cristiano was struggling to get the ball as a central striker, so he moved out wide in search of more space. From the right, he played a one-two and then slipped a great pass through to Diogo in the box. He swivelled brilliantly, but his shot flew just over the bar. *Missed!*

João Félix jumped up to win the header, but the result was a comfortable catch for Courtois. *Saved!*

Cristiano took another free kick, but he blasted it straight at the wall. *Blocked!*

Rúben Dias powered a header towards goal, but Courtois punched it away. *Saved!*

From the left side of the penalty area, Cristiano flicked the ball on for André Silva, but he couldn't quite reach it before the big Belgium keeper. *Saved again!*

When the final whistle blew, Cristiano screamed at the sky and then threw his captain's armband to the floor in frustration. Nooooo, not again! Despite his five goals, Portugal had once more failed to reach the quarter-finals of a major tournament, just like at the World Cups in 2014 and 2018.

What now – would Cristiano choose to end his incredible international career? No, even at the age of thirty-six, he was still determined to make it to one more World Cup in 2022. And before that, there was another big goal record that he really wanted to break.

PART 3

MAKING MORE FOOTBALL HISTORY

1 September 2021, Estádio Algarve

'Tonight's the night,' Cristiano told himself with confidence, leading Portugal out for their latest 2022 World Cup qualifier against the Republic of Ireland.

Only a few days earlier, he had completed a big move back to his old club, Manchester United, after twelve years away, but now, his mind was focused on captaining his country again. He had work to do: his team needed to win, and he needed to score.

With his fifth and final goal at Euro 2020, Cristiano now had a total of 109 goals, equalling the men's international record set by Iran's Ali Daei. Cristiano, however, wasn't the kind of person who was happy to share. No, he didn't want to be the joint-best; he wanted to be the single best, the 'GOAT', the greatest of all time. And this, Portugal's first match post-Euro 2020, was the perfect opportunity for him to break the record and make more football history.

Cristiano's first chance of the night arrived in only the ninth minute. As Bruno raced into the box to win the ball back, he was fouled by Irish midfielder Jeff Hendrick. *Penalty!*

There was no doubt whatsoever about who would take it. In fact, before Bruno even got up off the grass, Cristiano had already walked over and grabbed the ball. This was it: his big, history-making moment. After a puff of his cheeks, he moved forward with stuttering steps and then fired a powerful shot towards the bottom left corner…

…but the Irish keeper, Gavin Bazunu, had guessed the right way, and he blocked it with two strong hands. *SAVED!*

'Argghhhhh!' Cristiano winced as the ball was cleared away. First chance: wasted.

Oh well, surely it was only a matter of time? No, just before half-time, Ireland took a surprise lead and suddenly, Portugal were in World Cup qualification trouble. If they lost, Serbia would be on the same points as them with a game in hand, and only the top team in the group would go straight through to the tournament.

Força Portugal!

Diogo, Bruno and Bernardo all had decent chances to equalise, but with ten minutes left, they were still 1–0 down. Uh-oh, what an embarrassing defeat this would be! Unless their incredible captain could somehow save the day......

'Tonight's the night,' Cristiano told himself again with confidence. After his penalty miss, he owed his team a goal. From wide on the right wing, Gonçalo chipped a cross into the middle and Cristiano leapt high to meet it. BOOM! With the perfect mix of power and accuracy, he headed the ball down into the bottom corner. *1–1!*

Gooooooooooooooooooooaaaaaaaaaaaaaaaalllllllllllllll llllllllllll!!!!!!!!!!!!!!!!!!!

Number 110. Yessssss, he had done it; Cristiano had made more football history – he was now officially the single highest scorer of all time in men's international football!

There was no time for him to celebrate properly with a special 'Siuuuu!', however, because Portugal still had five more minutes to grab a winning goal. So instead, he raced straight back for the restart, while urging the fans to make more noise for their team.

Let's goooooooooooooo!

The next few minutes flew by without a shot, but in the fifth minute of injury time, João Mário managed to float one final cross into the Irish box. This was it: Portugal's last chance to score. The ball sailed just over André's head, but who was there in the right place at the right time, right behind him? Cristiano, of course! After sneaking back into an onside position, he jumped up between two defenders and guided an unstoppable header into the top corner. *2–1!*

Goooooooooooooooooooooaaaaaaaaaaaaaaaallllllllllllllll llllllllllll!!!!!!!!!!!!!!!!!!!

Number 111. Right, now he could really celebrate

properly! In his excitement, Cristiano even took his shirt off and threw it on the floor, before leaping into the air for...

'SIUUUU!'

As the fans cheered and his teammates threw their arms around him, Cristiano roared and roared. What a feeling and what a match! Portugal had fought back to win thanks to his two late goals, and he was the new number one scorer in the history of men's international football.

'Another historic night!' Cristiano posted proudly on social media. 'Unforgettable.'

PART 4

REACHING THE WORLD CUP THE HARD WAY

Thanks to that dramatic victory, Portugal stayed top of UEFA Qualification Group A, and a week later, their World Cup prospects looked even better. Because while they successfully beat Azerbaijan 3–0 without the suspended Cristiano, their rivals Serbia could only draw 1–1 with the Republic of Ireland. Hurray, now Portugal just had to win two of their last three games, and they would be on their way to Qatar!

1) Portugal 5 Luxembourg 0…

Win Number One! Playing in his 181st game for his country, a new European record, Cristiano Ronaldo scored two penalties in the first fifteen minutes and then completed his tenth international hat-trick with a late header.

SIUUUU!

So far, so simple, but Portugal's last two group matches looked a lot more difficult: Ireland away, and then Serbia at home. To get that one final victory they required, the team would need to stay focused and united, and they would probably need their incredible captain to score.

'We continue together in the ambition, in the dream,' Cristiano tweeted like a leader, 'to be present at the historic World Cup in Qatar in 2022!'

After some more heroic performances for his club, Manchester United, at last it was time for Cristiano to star for his country again. One more win: that's all Portugal needed now.

At home at the Aviva Stadium in Dublin, however, the Irish defence stood strong against them, and even Cristiano couldn't find a way past them. His best shot was bravely blocked by Séamus Coleman, and his best header bounced down just millimetres wide of the post.

'Noooooooooooooo!' Cristiano cried out, hiding

his frustrated face behind his hands. What a missed opportunity to win the game and book Portugal's place at the World Cup!

Unfortunately, the match finished 0–0, which meant they would have to at least draw with Serbia in their final group game. The good news was that Portugal would be playing at home in Lisbon; the bad news was that they would have to get the job done without their most experienced defender, Pepe, who had been sent off against Ireland. Was it time to start panicking? No – as long as they had Cristiano on the pitch, they would always be the favourites to win.

With the pressure on, Portugal got off to the perfect start. In the second minute, Bernardo raced in to win the ball off a Serbia midfielder and then set up Renato Sanches to score. *1–0!*

'Come onnnnn!' Cristiano cheered as he jogged over to join in the team celebrations. Surely, they were on their way to the World Cup now!

Or were they? Serbia soon recovered from the shock early goal, and as the game went on, they got better and better. First, Dušan Vlahović hit the post and then Dušan Tadić unleashed a fierce shot that Rui Patrício couldn't hold on to. It was 1–1 – game on!

Although a draw would still be enough to send Portugal through, they couldn't afford to just sit back and defend. Because what if Serbia scored again? That would be a disaster!

Besides, Cristiano didn't want to draw; he wanted to win. So he kept making clever forward runs, but the problem was that the ball never arrived.

'Yes!' he called out, but Renato's pass didn't quite reach him.

'Now!' he screamed, but Renato went for goal himself, and his shot flew straight at the Serbia keeper.

'Arghhhhh!' Cristiano threw his head back in frustration. He was in a much better position to score!

Oh well – as long as Portugal qualified for the World Cup, all would be forgiven and forgotten, but in the ninetieth minute, Serbia swung one last cross into the box and there was their super sub Aleksandar Mitrović, unmarked at the back post, to head the ball home. *2–1!*

Noooooooooooooooooooooo!

It was another head-in-hands moment for Cristiano. How on earth had they let this happen? The goal meant that Serbia had secured a spot at the World Cup, while Portugal would have to qualify the hard way, through the play-offs instead!

At the final whistle, Cristiano was absolutely furious, but eventually, he turned his anger and disappointment into action and determination. Yes, despite the disaster against Serbia, Portugal would still make it to the tournament in Qatar; he was going to make sure of that.

First up: a play-off semi-final against… Turkey.

Although Portugal's captain didn't score himself for once, he still played a key part in their victory.

In the first half, Cristiano poked the ball through to Diogo, who laid it back for Bernardo to shoot. His strike bounced back off the post and Otávio fired in the rebound. *1–0!*

'Yesssssssssss!' Cristiano cried out, throwing both arms in the air. That was more like it!

When Diogo scored a second goal just before half-time, Portugal seemed to be cruising to victory, but no, there was drama to come in the second half from the opposition. First, Burak Yilmaz made it 2–1, and then with five minutes to go, Turkey were awarded a penalty. Up stepped Yilmaz to equalise and… he smashed it over the bar!

The Portugal players breathed a big sigh of relief, and then raced up the other end and made it 3–1. Phew, play-off part one: won! They were now just one game away from the World Cup again.

'Força Portugal!' Cristiano tweeted. 'Let's go to Qatar!'

The last nation standing in their way were North Macedonia, the team ranked sixty-fourth in the world. That was fifty-five places lower than Portugal, but there was no way Cristiano was going to underestimate their opponents, especially not with a World Cup spot on the line.

In the thirteenth minute, Diogo threaded a great pass through to Cristiano, who looked certain to score. How many times had he fired the ball into the bottom corner from that position for Portugal? This time, however, he dragged his shot wide.

Noooooooooooooo!

Cristiano couldn't believe it, but he didn't let that miss drag him down. Twenty minutes later, he carried the ball forward and then laid it across to Bruno, who curled a shot into the bottom corner. *1–0!*

'Yesssssssssssssssss!' Cristiano shouted, lifting his arm in the air and then pointing at his teammate for club and country.

So far, so good – they were winning, but would they suffer another second-half setback? No, this time Bruno settled the nerves by scoring an all-important second goal. Hurray, Portugal had done it; they had reached the World Cup the hard way!

'Goal achieved,' Cristiano tweeted with great satisfaction. Now he couldn't wait for the main event in Qatar to kick off.

SADIO MANÉ

PART 1

2018: OUT OF THE WORLD CUP IN THE WORST POSSIBLE WAY

Starring in the Premier League – *Tick!*

Starring in the Champions League – *Tick!*

Sadio had achieved so much already in his football career, but which of his childhood dreams would come true next?

Starring at the World Cup with Senegal? Yes, because 'The Lions of Teranga' had successfully qualified for the 2018 tournament in Russia!

'Good luck!' Sadio joked with his Liverpool teammate Mo Salah, who was off to the World Cup too, to play for Egypt. 'May the best African country win!'

The two players' friendly rivalry had started when

they were both named on the shortlist for the African Footballer of the Year award. They had flown to Ghana together for the ceremony where the winner was announced...

'Mohamed Salah!'

'Well done, you deserve it,' Sadio congratulated his teammate sportingly. 'But let's see who wins at the World Cup!'

Senegal were aiming high in Russia. It would be their first appearance at the tournament since 2002, when The Lions of Teranga had shocked the world by beating the reigning champions France on their way through to the quarter-finals.

Could Super Senegal shine again, sixteen years later? Sadio and his teammates wouldn't get a better chance to follow in the footsteps of their childhood heroes. There weren't any top nations like France in their group this time. Instead, they would face Poland, Japan and Colombia.

'We can beat any of them!' Sadio declared confidently before their first match.

He couldn't wait to compete against world-class players like Robert Lewandowski and James Rodríguez. Sadio was now the Senegal captain and he wore the armband with great pride. As the national anthem played, he stood there with his hand on his heart and the team badge.

Senegal! Senegal! Senegal!

Just like in 2002, they got off to a winning start. Every time Senegal attacked, they looked so dangerous. Sadio wasn't playing on the left like he did for Liverpool; he was in the middle, creating chances for his team.

Ismaïla Sarr raced down the wing and passed inside to Sadio, who quickly shifted the ball across to Idrissa Gueye. His shot flicked off a Poland defender's boot and flew past the goalkeeper. 1–0!

'Wait, are you claiming that goal?' Sadio teased Idrissa as they celebrated.

'Of course, my shot was going in anyway!'

In the second half, Senegal secured the victory. Their striker M'Baye Niang sprinted after a bad backpass, beat the Poland goalkeeper to the ball and then passed it into the empty net. *2–0!*

'Brilliant work, M'Baye!' Sadio shouted happily, running over to hug their hero.

Next up: Japan. They had already shocked Colombia and they were looking to shock Senegal too. Their captain wasn't going to let that happen, however. As Youssouf Sabaly shot from the left, Sadio moved into the six-yard box, ready for the rebound. It was his lucky day; the Japan keeper spilled the ball and he was in the right place at the right time. *1–0!*

Gooooooooooooooooooooaaaaaaaaaaaaaaaaalllllllllllllll llllllllllll!!!!!!!!!!!!!!!!!!!!

It wasn't one of Sadio's best strikes, but that didn't matter. Senegal were 1–0 up and he had scored his first-ever World Cup goal. After all the hugs and high-fives from his teammates, he knelt down to kiss the ground. He was so grateful to be living his dream.

'Come on, stay focused!' Sadio clapped and cheered, returning to his role as captain.

But Japan fought back, not once but twice. *2–2!*

Although Sadio was pleased to win the man of the match award, he was disappointed with his team's result.

'We should have won that!' he told defender Kalidou Koulibaly, kicking the air in frustration.

If they wanted to succeed at the World Cup, Senegal couldn't give away two sloppy goals like that. They would all have to improve for their final group game, including their captain.

'Sadio Mané can do better,' his manager told the media, 'and he needs to do better against Colombia.'

Sadio was used to playing under pressure, but this was a new level of pressure. For his club, he was surrounded by other superstars: Mo, Roberto Firmino, Gini Wijnaldum, Jordan Henderson. For his country, however, he was the main man, and so everyone expected him to create magic all the time.

'I'm trying!' Sadio wanted to scream.

Winning Group H didn't look so straightforward anymore. Senegal and Japan both had four points, while Colombia had three. With one game to go, anything could happen!

Early in the first half, Keita Baldé threaded a lovely pass through to Sadio. As he burst into the box, the Colombia centre-back Davinson Sánchez stuck out a leg. Had he kicked the ball or Sadio's leg?

The referee pointed to the spot straight away. Penalty! But when he checked the VAR replays, he changed his mind. What drama!

'Keep going, forget about that!' captain Sadio clapped and cheered.

In the fifty-ninth minute, Poland took the lead against Japan.

Then in the seventy-third minute of their game, Colombia took the lead against Senegal. Sadio could only stand and watch on the edge of the area as Yerry Mina headed the ball home.

'Noooooo!' Sadio groaned, turning away in despair.

If things stayed the same, Colombia would win Group H with six points, and Japan and Senegal would be tied on the same points and the same goal difference. And in their head-to-head match, they had drawn 2–2. So, who would go through in second place? The answer was Japan, because of FIFA's 'Fair Play' rule. They had only picked up four yellow cards, compared to Senegal's six.

'No way!' Sadio wasn't giving up on his World Cup

dream just yet. Suddenly, he was all over the pitch, playing every position.

From the right wing, Sadio slipped a pass into M'Baye's path, but his shot was saved by the Colombia keeper.

'Noooooo!'

From the left wing, Sadio chipped a clever cross to Ismaïla at the back post. He was totally unmarked, but he blazed his volley high over the crossbar.

'Noooooo!'

In the middle, Sadio spun and fed the ball through to Moussa Konaté, but at the last second, Sánchez stuck out a leg to stop it.

'Noooooo!'

That was it – Senegal's last chance to score. It was over. They were out of the 2018 World Cup in the worst possible way.

'"Fair play"?' Sadio muttered moodily. 'There's nothing fair about that!'

He wanted to sit down and cry, but he was the captain of his country now, and he had to stay strong. So instead, he walked around comforting his teammates, telling them the same thing he had told Mo after Liverpool lost the 2018 Champions League Final against Real Madrid:

'We'll be back – just you wait and see!'

PART 2

BOUNCING BACK WITH CLUB AND COUNTRY

While he waited for his next chance to lead Senegal to glory, Sadio focused on finally lifting a trophy with Liverpool. Under manager Jürgen Klopp, the club was getting closer and closer to that target:

League Cup semi-finalists in 2017...

Then Champions League finalists in 2018...

'Come on, we've got to win something this year!' Sadio told his Liverpool teammates ahead of the 2018–19 season. Together, they were becoming a mean, winning machine, but they needed some silverware to prove it.

The League Cup? No, Liverpool lost to Chelsea.

The FA Cup? No, they were beaten by Wolves.

The Premier League? No, despite Mo and Sadio scoring twenty-two goals each, it was Manchester City who clinched the title on the final day. The difference between the two teams? Just one single point!

Arghhhhh!

It was so frustrating for the Liverpool players, but luckily there was still one trophy left for them to win: the Champions League!

Yes, against all odds, Liverpool had bounced back from that defeat to Real Madrid to reach their second final in a row, and Sadio had played a very important part. After a quiet group stage, he had stepped up to become a big game hero again in the knock-out rounds.

He scored two great goals to beat Bayern Munich in the Last 16...

Got a goal and an assist against Porto in the quarters...

And then, with Mo and Roberto both out injured, Sadio helped lead Liverpool to a miraculous comeback against Barcelona in the semis. From 3–0 down in the first leg, they bounced back to win 4–0 at Anfield and reach the Champions League final again!

There, they faced their English rivals, Tottenham. They had a strong team with stars like Harry Kane, Son Heung-min and Christian Eriksen, but Sadio was sure that Liverpool could beat them, especially if they got off to a really good start…

Seconds after kick-off, Sadio was already causing chaos in the Tottenham defence. From just inside the box, he tried to play a pass to Jordan, but the ball struck Moussa Sissoko's arm instead. Penalty!

'Come on!' Sadio roared with both joy and relief. The 2019 final was already looking a whole lot better than that of 2018.

Liverpool didn't look back after that. Mohamed scored the spot-kick and then with five minutes to go, Divock made it 2–0.

'We did it,' Sadio cheered at the final whistle. 'WE'RE THE CHAMPIONS OF EUROPE!'

It was the perfect end to his best-ever season: twenty-six goals, five assists, and most exciting of all, one gigantic, glittering Champions League trophy.

Well, it was the perfect end to his club season,

anyway. But a few weeks later, Sadio was setting off for Egypt to captain his country at the 2019 Africa Cup of Nations. Two years earlier, his tournament had ended in tears and misery after he missed the crucial penalty in Senegal's quarter-final shoot-out against Cameroon. Now, it was time for Sadio to bounce back and become a hero, just like he had with Liverpool.

GOAL! GOAL! In Senegal's important final group game against Kenya, he scored twice to secure the victory, including one from the penalty spot.

'Come onnnnnnnnn!' Sadio roared with joy and relief. He was back, back to his magical best.

In the Round of 16, he was Senegal's matchwinner again. After collecting a pass from M'Baye, Sadio dribbled into the Uganda box and calmly guided the ball into the bottom corner. *1–0!*

Goooooooooooooooooooaaaaaaaaaaaaaaaalllllllllllllll llllllllllll!!!!!!!!!!!!!!!!!!!

Sadio was on fire, but could he lead Senegal past the quarter-finals this time and through to the semi-finals? Yes! In the crowded space outside the Benin penalty area, he used his quick feet to escape from three defenders and then poked a clever pass through to Idrissa. *1–0!*

Hurrrraaaaaaaaaaaaaayyyyy!

'The Lions of Teranga' were now just two games away from winning the Africa Cup of Nations for the first time ever. As the excitement grew across the country, captain Sadio did his best to keep his players calm. Senegal had to take things step by step, starting with a tough semi-final against Tunisia.

It was a tight game with very few goalscoring chances, but in the seventy-fifth minute, Tunisia were awarded a penalty. Uh-oh – was Senegal's trophy dream in serious danger? No, because their keeper Alfred Gomis stayed strong and saved the spot-kick.

'Yessssssssssss!' Sadio screamed with passion – his team were still in the semi-final!

Inspired by the penalty save, Senegal pushed forward on the attack and five minutes later, they won a spot-kick of their own. The supporters were expecting Sadio to place the ball down on the spot, but no, after that painful miss against Cameroon, he decided to give it to Henri Saivet instead, who stepped up to score, but it was … *SAVED AGAIN!*

'Noooooooooo!' Sadio groaned, with his head in his hands. He really should have just taken it himself!

Eventually, however, after a mistake from the Tunisia keeper in extra-time, Senegal still won the match and made it through to the final. Phew, their dream was still alive!

To be crowned the new Champions of Africa, however, Senegal would have to win against Algeria, the team that had beaten them 1–0 in the group stage. In the battle of the Premier League superstars, it was Sadio versus Manchester City winger Riyad Mahrez. So, which leader would lift the trophy?

When the big final kicked off, Senegal got off to a seriously unlucky start. There didn't seem to be much danger as Algeria striker Baghdad Bounedjah dribbled the ball forward, but his shot deflected off defender Salif Sané's leg, looped up over Alfred's head, and landed in the back of the net. 1–0!

What?! How?! Sadio couldn't believe what he'd just seen. In only the second minute of the match, his team had just conceded the flukiest goal ever. Oh well, at least, they had lots of time to fight back...

Late in the first half, M'Baye hit a fierce shot that seemed to be heading for the top corner, but no, it flew just over the bar.

Ooooooooohhhh!

In the second half, Sadio grew more and more determined to save the day for Senegal. His country was counting on him! He kept running and dribbling, trying to create some space, but when he did manage to spin away from his marker and fire the ball into the middle, the Algeria defence cleared it away.

Aaaaaaaaahhhhh!

It just wasn't Senegal's day. In the sixtieth minute, they were awarded another penalty, but after checking the replays on the screen, the referee changed his mind.

Come onnnnnnn!

The minutes rushed by until – just as Salif's free kick cannoned straight into the wall – the final whistle blew. It was all over, and it was more heartbreak for Senegal. Sadio sat there on the pitch with his head between his legs, as the Algeria players celebrated around him.

Although it was devastating to get so close to glory, Sadio eventually picked himself up and focused on the positives. His Senegal team had made real progress by reaching the Africa Cup of Nations final, and they had many more major tournaments ahead.

PART 3

SADIO VS MO PART 1: AFRICA CUP OF NATIONS

6 February 2022, Olembe Stadium, Cameroon

Nearly three years on from that defeat to Algeria, Sadio and Senegal were back in the Africa Cup of Nations final, taking on Egypt.

This time, Kalidou was wearing the captain's armband, but Sadio was still Senegal's star man in attack. His three goals and two assists had helped lead the team all the way through to the final again.

And this time, in the battle of the Premier League superstars, it was Sadio versus his friend and club teammate Mo. So, which of Liverpool's fantastic forwards would lift the trophy?

Early on, Senegal's left-back Saliou Ciss made a bursting run into the box, where he was fouled by an Egypt defender. *Penalty!*

Wow, what a start it would be if Sadio could score! Yes, this time, he wasn't letting anyone else take the spot-kick; this was his responsibility. So what if he had missed penalties in the past? This was his chance to put things right and become Senegal's hero.

After gulping down some water, Sadio ran up and blasted the ball low towards the bottom left corner. But thanks to some advice from Mo, the Egypt keeper dived the right way and managed to block the shot. *SAVED!*

Nooooooooooooooo!

On the inside, Sadio felt crushed, but he didn't let it show. Instead, he just got on with the game. All he could do now was keep working hard and try to make up for his miss...

Twice Ismaïla crossed the ball from the right, and twice Sadio couldn't quite reach it with his outstretched left leg. But rather than getting angry and frustrated, he gave his teammate a thumbs-up and kept on going.

Then in the second half, Sadio had an even better chance to score. As the ball bounced to him in the six-yard box, he just had to keep calm and shoot, but his first touch was too heavy and the keeper quickly grabbed the ball back.

NOOOOOOOOOOOO!

In that moment, it seemed like Sadio and Senegal were destined to lose another Africa Cup of Nations final, but Egypt couldn't score either, and so after extra-time, the match went all the way to...

PENALTIES!

Oh dear – would Sadio be brave enough to step up to the spot again? Of course, he was willing to do anything to win a trophy for his country, and to make up for his earlier miss. Before the shoot-out began, he knelt down and kissed the grass for good luck. Then he walked around encouraging his tired and anxious teammates.

'Come on, we can win this!'

As Senegal's most experienced player, Sadio was asked to take the fifth and final penalty. That meant a lot of pressure and a lot of watching and waiting:

Scored,

Scored,

Scored,

Saved,

Saved,

Scored,

Scored,

SAVED!

When Sadio finally made the long journey forward from the halfway line, it was all set up for him to become the hero. Because if he scored, Senegal would be crowned the new Champions of Africa.

It sounded so simple, but really it was much more complicated than that. Sadio was playing in a major final, and so he had the nerves and the pressure to deal with, as well as the painful memories of previous missed penalties.

As he carefully placed the ball down on the spot, however, he focused his mind fully on the task in front of him. All he had to do was beat the keeper and the trophy would be theirs.

But what should he do – aim for the same side as last time, or go the other way? After a long run-up, he fired the ball low and to the left again. The Egypt keeper dived that way too, but this time, Sadio's strike was so powerful and accurate that it couldn't be stopped.

Goooooooooooooooooooooaaaaaaaaaaaaaaaaalllllllllllllll llllllllllll!!!!!!!!!!!!!!!!!!!!!!

He had done it; they had done it – for the first time ever, Senegal were the Champions of Africa! Before he knew it, Sadio was at the bottom of a big pile of ecstatic teammates. What a feeling! After missing a penalty earlier in the match, he had bounced back to become a national hero.

Even in that amazing moment, however, Sadio still remembered to show respect for his opponents, and one player in particular.

'I'm sorry, my friend,' he said, putting a comforting arm around Mo's shoulder on the pitch. 'Well played – you'll be back.'

Right, where was that trophy? As he went up to collect his winners' medal, Sadio had a huge smile on his face and a green, yellow and red Senegal scarf around his neck. On the way, he walked past the golden trophy, and he couldn't help picking it up to take a closer look. Wow, what a beauty! He couldn't wait to lift it properly.

Eventually every Senegal player had their medal and their captain Kalidou had the trophy in his hands. It was time for the real celebrations to start.

'Ready?' he called out to his teammates.

'Yessssssssssssssssssssss!' they all replied.

Then with a lion's roar, Kalidou lept up and raised the cup towards the sky.

Hurrraaaaaaaaaaaaayyyyyyyyyyyyyyyyyyy!

That night, the singing and dancing went on and on, both in the stadium in Cameroon, and also back home in the streets of Senegal. Their historic victory had helped to bring the whole nation together, from the capital city Dakar to Sadio's little boyhood village of Bambali.

Sometimes when he stopped to think, he couldn't believe how far he had come and how much he had achieved already during his football career: the

Champions League trophy, the Premier League title and now the Africa Cup of Nations too.

'Dreams come true,' Sadio wrote on social media the next day, alongside a photo of him kissing the trophy. He was so proud of his team's success, but why stop there? Although 'Champions of Africa' had a very nice ring to it, 'Champions of the World' sounded even better!

PART 4

SADIO VS MO PART 2: WORLD CUP QUALIFICATION

29 March 2022, Stade Léopold Sédar Senghor,
Senegal

Time for Round Two! Less than two months after the
Africa Cup of Nations final, Sadio's Senegal faced Mo's
Egypt again in another two massive matches. This
time, there was no trophy up for grabs, but the prize
for the winner was very precious indeed – a place at
the 2022 World Cup in Qatar.

Sadio was desperate to play at football's greatest
tournament again, but after a 1–0 defeat away in
Egypt, Senegal returned home with work to do in the
second leg. One goal would take the tie to extra-time,

and two would take them to the World Cup, just as long as Egypt didn't score any of their own.

When the big game kicked off, it only took Senegal four minutes to equalise. As the ball bounced around the box, striker Boulaye Dia fired it goalwards and it deflected in off a defender. *1–1!*

Hurrrraaaaayyyyyyyyyy!

It wasn't the prettiest of moves, but that didn't matter to Sadio and his teammates as they celebrated together. They were level, and with luck on their side, they were halfway to Qatar!

Now, could they go on and win the game? With ten minutes left, Sadio created a golden chance for Senegal. Collecting the ball in the pocket of space between the Egypt defence and midfield, he slipped a brilliant pass through to Ismaïla as he raced into the box. One on one with the keeper, he curled his shot... wide of the far post.

Noooooooooooo! Other Senegal players threw their hands to their heads in disappointment, but not Sadio. He just calmly carried on looking for another way to lead his country to the World Cup.

As the last of the ninety minutes ticked by, both teams were still searching for a winning goal, but who would get it – Senegal or Egypt? And who would be the hero – Sadio or Mo?

Early in extra-time, Sadio raced up the left wing, beat the Egypt right-back with a lovely stepover, and then swept the ball across the six-yard box towards the back post, where Ismaïla was running in. Surely, this was it – the winning goal to send Senegal to the World Cup? But no, from really close range, Ismaïla somehow hit his shot straight at the keeper. *SAVED!*

Noooooooooooo, Senegal and Egypt were going all the way to penalties again! As the nerves began to set in, Sadio walked around high-fiving his teammates with calm confidence. They had beaten Egypt in a shoot-out before, so of course they could do it again!

A few doubts did creep in when Kalidou and Saliou both missed for Senegal, but fortunately for them, Egypt couldn't score either. First, Mo shocked everyone by blazing his shot high over the bar, and then Zizo fired wide. *Phew!* Senegal were still in the shoot-out, and Ismaïla went next, making up for his earlier misses by scoring from the spot.

'Yessssss, come on!' Sadio clapped and cheered on the halfway line. When he finally made the long journey forward to take his team's fifth and final penalty, the situation was the same as in the Africa Cup of Nations final. If he scored, he would be the hero and Senegal would be the winners.

Sadio didn't look like a player under pressure, though, as he spun the ball between his hands and then carefully placed it down on the spot. After another long run-up, he blasted a shot straight down the middle, while the keeper dived to his left.

Gooooooooooooooooooooaaaaaaaaaaaaaaaaalllllllllllllll llllllllllll!!!!!!!!!!!!!!!!!!!

It was all over, and Sadio and Senegal were on their way to the World Cup! With his arms stretched out wide, he raced away to celebrate with his teammates in front of the fans. Together, they had achieved another goal: taking their country to another World Cup.

What an incredible year 2022 was turning out to be for 'The Lions of Teranga', and the best part –

football's greatest tournament – was still to come in November. The next day, once the party was over, Sadio went on social media to send out an exciting message to his fans:

'Qatar, I am coming with my Lions. See you soon.'

EPILOGUE

Doha Exhibition and Convention Center, Qatar
1 April 2022

It was the moment that the football heroes had been waiting for. After all the games, the goals and the hard work to qualify, finally it was time for the thirty-two successful teams to find out who they would be up against in the World Cup group stage come November. The draw was taking place on a stage in Qatar, but there were fans and footballers watching with interest all over the world.

'In Group A...,' announced the presenters, allowing a long, dramatic pause as former Qatar international

Adel Ahmed Malalla picked out a ball from the bowl, opened up the paper inside, and held it up to the TV cameras: '...Senegal!'

The Lions of Teranga would be taking on the hosts Qatar, as well as Ecuador and the Netherlands.

'We can beat any of them!' Sadio declared confidently, as he had back in 2018.

'In Group B...,' the presenters continued. It was legendary Brazil defender Cafu's turn to hold up the next name and he did so with a big smile on his face: '...England!'

Their first-round opponents would be the USA, Iran and their British rivals, Wales.

'I'll take that,' Declan said as he discussed the draw with his best mate Mason. 'Bring it on!'

On the stage in Qatar, Cafu carried on picking out the top-seeded teams:

'In Group C... Argentina!'

La Albiceleste would be up against Poland, Mexico and Saudi Arabia.

'Our journey starts now, vamos!' Lionel sent out to his fans on social media.

'In Group D... France!'

For Kylian and his teammates, it was a case of déjà vu because *Les Bleus* were in the same group as two of their first-round opponents from the tournament in 2018: Denmark and Australia! No problem – they would just have to battle their way past both of them again, and Tunisia too.

'In Group F... Belgium!'

The Red Devils had been drawn with Croatia, Morocco and Canada.

'Right, let's show the world why we're the number one-ranked team!' Kevin told Romelu and Eden.

'And finally, in Group H... Portugal!'

They would be facing Uruguay, Ghana and South Korea. Although it wasn't quite the 'Group of Death' that Portugal had experienced at Euro 2020, there would still be challenging times ahead against top players like Edinson Cavani, Iñaki Williams, and Son Heung-min. With Cristiano on the pitch, however, anything felt possible.

Thirty-two teams, eight groups, and one glittering gold trophy up for grabs – the heroes had reached the end of the Road to the 2022 World Cup. Soon, it would be time for the main event to kick off in Qatar. There could only be one winner. Who would it be?

Football's greatest tournament – was still to come in November. The next day, once the party was over, Sadio went on social media to send out an exciting message to his fans:

'Qatar, I am coming with my Lions. See you soon.'

TOURNAMENT PLANNER

We've been waiting for this moment for four years, but the 2022 World Cup is finally here! Fill in the tables over the page when all the group games have been played, then continue on with the round of 16, quarter-finals and semi-finals to plot the path to the World Cup final!

P = Played   F = Goals for
W = Won   A = Goals against
D = Drawn   Pts = Points
L = Lost

GROUP STAGE

GROUP A	P	W	D	L	F	A	PTS
Qatar							
Ecuador							
Senegal							
Netherlands							

GROUP B	P	W	D	L	F	A	PTS
England							
Iran							
USA							
Wales							

GROUP C	P	W	D	L	F	A	PTS
Argentina							
Saudi Arabia							
Mexico							
Poland							

GROUP D	P	W	D	L	F	A	PTS
France							
Denmark							
Tunisia							
Australia							

GROUP E	P	W	D	L	F	A	PTS
Spain							
Germany							
Japan							
Costa Rica							

GROUP F	P	W	D	L	F	A	PTS
Belgium							
Canada							
Morocco							
Croatia							

GROUP G	P	W	D	L	F	A	PTS
Brazil							
Serbia							
Switzerland							
Cameroon							

GROUP H	P	W	D	L	F	A	PTS
Portugal							
Ghana							
Uruguay							
South Korea							

LAST 16

The winner and the runner-up of each group go through to the Round of 16. Fill in the teams and the scores below.

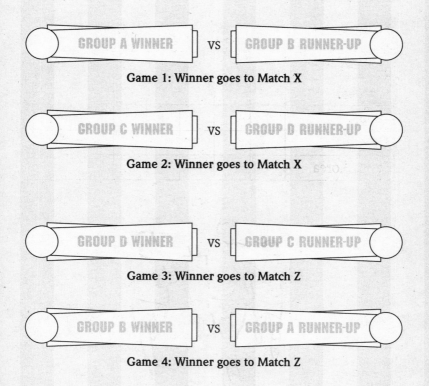

GROUP A WINNER   vs   GROUP B RUNNER-UP

Game 1: Winner goes to Match X

GROUP C WINNER   vs   GROUP D RUNNER-UP

Game 2: Winner goes to Match X

GROUP D WINNER   vs   GROUP C RUNNER-UP

Game 3: Winner goes to Match Z

GROUP B WINNER   vs   GROUP A RUNNER-UP

Game 4: Winner goes to Match Z

GROUP E WINNER VS GROUP F RUNNER-UP

Game 5: Winner goes to Match W

GROUP G WINNER VS GROUP H RUNNER-UP

Game 6: Winner goes to Match W

GROUP F WINNER VS GROUP E RUNNER-UP

Game 7: Winner goes to Match Y

GROUP H WINNER VS GROUP G RUNNER-UP

Game 8: Winner goes to Match Y

QUARTER FINALS

Fill in the teams from the previous rounds in the
boxes and add the scores when the game is over.

Match W · Winner goes to Match I

GAME 1 WINNER   VS   GAME 2 WINNER

Match X · Winner goes to Match I

GAME 3 WINNER   VS   GAME 4 WINNER

Match Y · Winner goes to Match II

GAME 5 WINNER   VS   GAME 6 WINNER

Match Z · Winner goes to Match II

GAME 7 WINNER   VS   GAME 8 WINNER

SEMI FINALS

Nearly there – the winners of these go to the
finals, the loser to the third place match.

Match I · Winner goes to Final

| GAME W WINNER | VS | GAME X WINNER |

Match II · Winner goes to Final

| GAME Y WINNER | VS | GAME Z WINNER |

THE 2022 WORLD CUP FINAL

| GAME I WINNER | VS | GAME II WINNER |

TOURNAMENT SUMMARY CHART

When it's all over, you can fill in all the details.
How did your team do? Did you support a World Cup-
winning team, or is it a case of better luck next time?

Winner _____

Runner-up _____

Third place _____

Fourth place _____

Golden boot _____

Goal of the tournament scored by _____

Best match _____

Number of goals scored _____

Number of yellow cards _____

Number of red cards _____

DESIGN YOUR OWN SHIRT

Here is your chance to make up your very own shirt.
This could be a special edition for your school team,
the team you support, or your family football team.
Use the space below to draw in the details.
You can have advertising if you like,
to make it look really professional!

DRAW YOUR OWN BADGE

Now you will need your own football team badge
to go on your lovely new shirt. Use the space below
to design it – think about how it will look when it is
small on a shirt – and colour it in when you are done.
Use family or football imagery, or things that
relate to the city or countryside around
you to make it look really special.

FUN FOOTBALL FACTS

EARLY DAYS

The first ever World Cup was held
in Uruguay in 1930. Only four teams
from Europe attended: Belgium, France,
Romania and Yugoslavia, and no teams from Africa
or Asia were there. The United States came third!

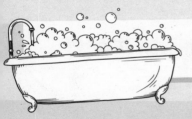

(VERY) EARLY BATH

In 1986 Uruguay's José Batista
was sent off after less than a minute in a
World Cup match against Scotland. After only fifty-
six seconds on the pitch, he made a tackle that the
referee deemed worthy of a red card. Scotland were
unable to take advantage though; they drew 0–0
and still ended up bottom of their group.

EVER-PRESENT

The Mexico national team has qualified for
the World Cup finals sixteen times. They have never
won it, and the furthest they progressed was
to the quarter-finals in 1970 and 1986 – both years
they were hosts. They are co-hosts with the USA
in 2026 so will be hoping for more success.

NEVER-PRESENT

South Korea holds the
unwanted record for being
eliminated the most times in the first round of the
World Cup. Before any England fans laugh,
remember that your team holds the record
for quarter-final eliminations!

GOAL MACHINE

French player Just Fontaine scored thirteen goals in one World Cup, in 1958. Amazingly this only puts him fourth on the list of World Cup top-scorers. The record for goals in one match is held by Russia's Oleg Salenko, who scored five against Cameroon in 1994.

SORE BACK

In 1954, the South Korean goalkeeper picked up the unwanted record of having the most goals scored against a team. Despite only playing two matches, Hong Duk-Yung (and his team) conceded sixteen times. Admittedly, nine of those came in their match against Hungary and they only lost their match against Turkey 0–7, so you could call that progress!

TOURNAMENT DREAM TEAM

Every major championship has a team of the tournament. This is made up of the players who have performed the best throughout. It's not always made up of all the members of the winning team though, usually there are players from many teams in it. Fill in the names for the players below, and check out the news to find out what the football pundits think – did they make the same choices as you?

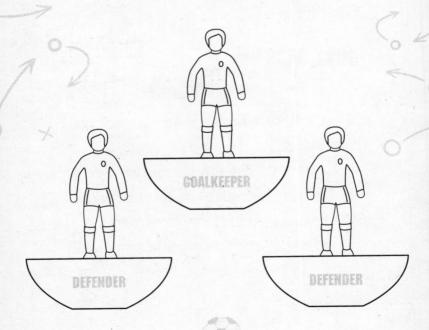

GOALKEEPER

DEFENDER

DEFENDER

WORLD CUP BY NUMBERS

45

The oldest player ever at a World Cup was Essam El Hadary. He played in the 2018 World Cup in Russia as goalkeeper for the Egyptian national team. He even saved a penalty, making him the oldest penalty-saver at a World Cup too!

12

The most goals scored in a world cup match, not including shoot-outs. Austria beat Switzerland 7–5 at the 1954 World Cup, where Switzerland were hosts!

Only two teams have won the World Cup twice in a row: Italy (1934 & 1938) and Brazil (1958 & 1962). France and Germany both won the tournament but were dumped out of the following World Cups in the group stages.

2

The most World Cup goals scored by a single player. Germany's Miroslav Klose scored these across four World Cups, between 2002 and 2014. He is also the German national team's all-time record goal-scorer.

The number of teams in the first World Cup in Uruguay, in 1930. There was one group of four teams and three groups of three. Uruguay beat Argentina in the final, but a different ball was used in each half of that match because the teams could not agree on a 'neutral' ball.

Yes, that's three and a half billion. That's the number of people who watched the World Cup Final in 2018. That was roughly half the population of the world at the time!

FAMOUS FORMATIONS

I know it looks to some people like twenty-two players running around a pitch kicking a ball, but a vast amount of research goes into the way the teams line up and the space they occupy on a pitch. This has evolved over the years, and here are some of the significant formations that have been popular...

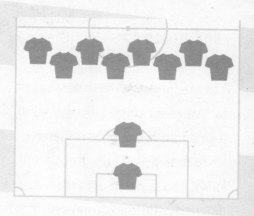

1 – 1 – 8

It seems almost impossible today to think that a football team would line up with one defender, one midfielder and eight forwards (unless we're talking about Norwich City) but this was a common formation in the 19th century.

W – M

The attack was the W and the defence was the M in this seemingly complicated, hugely modern system that was popularised by the legendary Herbert Chapman at Arsenal in the 1930s. It was still popular in 1950, with a few World Cup teams playing this way, but not the way eventual winners Uruguay played. Maybe not a surprise it faded out then...

CHRISTMAS TREE

There's nothing festive about this formation! It's also known as 4–3–2–1 and it's a very defensive style, allowing solidity in the defence and not, hopefully, a gift for the opposition!

4 – 4 – 2

One of the most used – and adapted – football formations, this is still very popular in the modern game, particularly in England. In order to be successful, it requires hard work and a strong team ethic, with players covering a lot of the pitch. Some grumpy fans would say it's no wonder England haven't won a World Cup since 1966!

QUIZ TIME!

Test your knowledge of the beautiful game with this quiz and circle the correct answers. When you've had a go why not test your nearest and dearest too?

1 What legendary player famously called football 'the beautiful game'?

A. Danny Blanchflower
B. Pelé

C. Queen Elizabeth II
D. Vinny Jones

2 In what year was the first world cup?

A. 1800
B. 1900
C. 1930
D. 1950

3 Which country won the first world cup?

A. Argentina
B. Brazil
C. Italy
D. Uruguay

4 Laeeb is the mascot of the 2022 World Cup. Which of the following was NOT an official mascot in a previous tournament?

A. Footix
B. Soccerboi

C. World Cup Willie
D. Zakumi

5 Sadio Mané played for Liverpool in the Premier League in 2021, but which team did he sign for in the summer of 2022?

A. Bayern Munich
B. Chelsea
C. Dallas Cowboys
D. Paris Saint-Germain

6 Kylian Mbappé chose to stay in his native France at Paris Saint-Germain. But which team did he play for professionally first, aged only 16?

A. Le Havre AC   C. Red Star FC
B. Monaco   D. Stade Rennais

7 Lionel Messi made his name at Barcelona in Spain, but which of the following teams did he first play for as a youth in Argentina?

A. Boca Juniors   C. River Plate
B. Newell's Old Boys D. Santos

8 Which of the following teams has Cristiano Ronaldo NOT played for?

A. Manchester United C. Sporting Lisbon
B. Real Madrid D. A.C. Milan

9 Which Premier League team did Kevin de Bruyne play for before Manchester City?

A. Arsenal C. Chelsea
B. Brentford D. Manchester United

10 Declan Rice is a regular for the England team, but once he played for another national team. Which was it?

A. Northern Ireland C. Scotland
B. Republic of Ireland D. Wales

11 One team has won the World Cup more than once but didn't make it to Qatar 2022. Which one?

A. Brazil

B. Czech Republic

C. Italy

D. Russia

12 FIFA ranks all international football teams. The number one spot is often occupied by Brazil, but do you know which team in the 2022 World Cup has the lowest ranking?

A. Australia

B. Costa Rica

C. Qatar

D. Saudi Arabia

13 England played the world's first international match, but did not feel like entering the World Cup until which year?

A. 1938

B. 1950

C. 1954

D. 1986

14 And in England's first World Cup, the team infamously lost 1–0 to a team that they were expected to beat. Who was it?

A. Hungary   C. Italy
B. Iceland   D. USA

15 There have been more than fifteen England managers since an individual took over from the International Select Committee. Which of the following was an actual England national team manager?

A. Bert Birkenstock   C. Marty Matchwinner
B. George Goalscorer   D. Walter Winterbottom

16 England's finest hour in the World Cup came in 1966, when they won at Wembley. But do you know how many World Cup semi-finals the England national team has won?

A. 0   B. 1   C. 2   D. 3

NICKNAMES

Can you match the nicknames on the left
with the teams on the right?

A Seleção	**Wales**
Black Stars	Brazil
Clockwork Orange	**Argentina**
Die Mannschaft	South Korea
The Dragons	**England**
Indomitable Lions	Cameroon
La Albiceleste	**Australia**
Lions of Teranga	Germany
Socceroos	**Netherlands**
Taegeuk Warriors	Senegal
The Three Lions	**Ghana**

DRIBBLE CHALLENGE

The four players below are all taking a shot on goal, but only one has the skills to hit the target and put their team a goal ahead. Follow the amazing trajectory of the ball to see which player gets the goal!

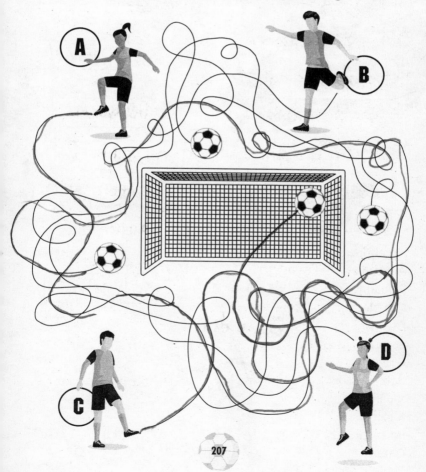

WHERE IN THE WORLD?

A. canada

E. Denmark

F. Belgium

G. Portugal

B. mexico

H. tunsia

I. ghana

C. Ecuador

D. argentina

Argentina
Australia
Belgium
Canada
Denmark
Ecuador
Ghana
Iran
Japan
Mexico
Portugal
Qatar
Tunisia

Teams at the World Cup come from, duh, all over the world. We've highlighted some of the World Cup qualifying countries on the map but missed out the names. Can you identify the countries and fill them in?

J _Iran_

L _Japan_

K _Qatar_

M _Australia_

THE LANGUAGE OF FOOTBALL

1 S h o T

An attempt to put the ball in the net.

2 P E n a l t Y

Also known as a spot-kick, a free attempt on goal from twelve yards, with only the keeper to beat.

3 O f f i D E

One of the most complicated rules to explain, this happens when a player receives a pass but is too far ahead of the game.

4 f R e e K i C k

When a player has broken a rule and is told off by the ref, the other team usually gets one of these.

5 C O r ʌ E R

If the ball goes out of play at the end of the pitch, you could be awarded one of these.

Football, or soccer as some call it, comes with its own language and special terms. Can you work out the term from the definition given below?

6 I H r o w **I N**

If the ball goes out of play on the side of the pitch, one of the teams will be awarded one of these.

7 r E f a r e e

The person who is supposed to keep the match in order and keep play going...

8 S t r I k e r

This is the person you expect to score the most goals.

9 O w **N** G o a L

In football, scoring is great, unless it's at your end of the pitch. If you do that, it's an...

10 r e d **c** a r d

If you are very naughty on a football pitch, you may earn yourself one of these from the person in charge.

MEMORABLE MOMENTS

The World Cup has brought joy, excitement and amazing football to the world's population for nearly 100 years. And in that time, there have been some very memorable occurrences. Here we look at a few. Hopefully 2022 will have some additions to the list!

GOOD DIEGO, 1986

Argentinian football legend Diego Maradona was without a doubt one of the greatest players ever (ask someone over 40). In 1986 he pretty much single-handedly dribbled past most of the England team and calmly slotted home against Peter Shilton, one of the world's best keepers at the time. It was an incredible show of skill and bravado from a unique player.

BAD DIEGO, 1986

This was an example of the other side of Maradona – he could be a very naughty boy. In an aerial challenge with Peter Shilton (poor old Pete – what did he do to deserve this?), the rather short Argentinian player got to the ball before Shilts, who was a lot taller. It turned out that rather than an amazing jump, Maradona used his hand, and in the days before VAR there was nothing to be done, and the goal he scored afterwards was allowed to stand. The England camp wasn't happy, and most people have never forgotten what came to be known as the "Hand of God" (that's how Maradona described it afterwards, the cheeky scamp).

KUWAIT DON'T WAIT, 1982

In a rather extraordinary turn of events, the entire Kuwaiti team left the field of play after their defenders thought they heard a whistle and stood still while France scored a goal, which the ref awarded. The team was so annoyed that they walked off. They did come back but lost the match 4–1.

NO GOAL GOAL, 1978

Sweden were playing against a powerful Brazil side in 1978, and the score was 1–1 right at the end, when Brazil scored from a corner. Or so they thought. As the goal-scorer Zico celebrated, the ref informed both teams that he had blown the whistle while the ball was kicked in, so it wouldn't count. And it didn't.

MWEPA MADNESS, 1974

In a match between Brazil (well, to be fair they do tend to always qualify and usually do well) and Zaire, Brazil were awarded a free kick. As both teams lined up, ready and waiting with the ball placed, Zaire's Mwepa Ilunga ran out from the wall and booted the ball upfield towards Brazil's goal. Search it up and have a look – it's really odd. Incidentally, that was the last time Zaire (now DR Congo) qualified for a World Cup. They also lost 9–0 to Yugoslavia, but that's another story...

CRUYFF DOES A CRUYFF TURN, 1974

You have to be a pretty good player to have a move named after you, and that is indeed the case with the Netherlands' Johan Cruyff. He was playing against Sweden and at one point seemed to have nowhere to go. But a turn, a spin and a flick later, he was bearing down on goal: the *Cruyff Turn* was born.

SPOT THE DIFFERENCE

Look at the exciting football scenes below.
Can you spot ten differences between the two?

ANAGRAMS

Can you work out who the players are from these mix-ups of their names?

Harry Kane

 (1) YAH RANKER

cristiano ronaldo

(2) ANTICORROSION LAD

 (3) ABEL MANKY PIP

(4) BLONDIE WATERWORKS

 (5) SIMEON ELLIS

(6) DUKE NERVY BENI

(7) DIANE AMOS

 (8) NIHILISTIC CARPUS

(9) MOE SHUNNING

 (10) CECIL ARDEN

QATAR 2022:
WHAT TO LOOK FOR

Qatar has never hosted a World Cup before (Qatar has never even *qualified* for a World Cup before), so it's a great opportunity to make new friends and learn about this country. Here's a few things to watch out for.

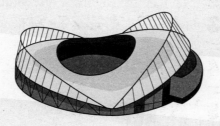

TIME DIFFERENCE

Qatar is two hours ahead of the UK, so the first match kicks off at 10am if you are in England, Wales, Scotland or Northern Ireland. That means if you're at school that day you may have to ask nicely if you want to watch — that means you too, Mr Jenkins!

WHEN IN ROME...

In local Qatari culture, male and female visitors are expected to show respect to the locals by covering up in public. This may have an effect on what we see fans wearing in the stadiums, especially those guys who paint letters on their naked torsos! Also, drinking alcohol is forbidden in public so there will be fewer over-happy fans too.

HOT OR NOT?

The average temperature in Qatar in December is only 24 degrees centigrade, a bit like a warm summer's day in the UK. It's just as well they didn't arrange it for their summer – the average temperature in July is an ice-cream melting 42°C! There's not much rain though, so expect plenty of water breaks for players, match officials and fans.

NOT FAR TO GO

All eight of the World Cup 2022 stadiums are within an hour's drive of Qatar's capital city, Doha. Let's hope the expected 1,500,000 visiting football fans won't spend all their time in traffic jams! In order to accommodate the extra tourism in the country, two huge luxury liners have docked in Doha Port, and will act as floating hotels.

WHO'S YOUR FAVOURITE?

The tournament favourites are (as usual) Brazil, England and France but that does not mean there won't be a surprise package in there somewhere. Only eight countries have ever won the world cup, and seven of them will be in Qatar in December, hoping to pick it up again. Only Italy – current UEFA Euro champions – are missing.

WINTER BREAK?

Some European leagues have a winter break from football (Germany stops for a month, France for more than three weeks) and sometimes even Scottish teams take a long break from the game. In England, however, there's no rest and it is traditional to have a match on Boxing Day. This year, however, there will be a much longer break than the usual three days(!), as players make their way to Qatar. With the World Cup final played just before Christmas and Premier League fixtures starting again on Boxing Day, expect some tired legs in January!

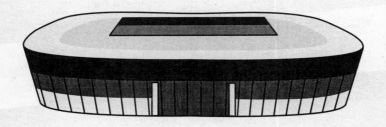

ANSWERS

QUIZ TIME:

1.	B	5.	A	9.	C	13.	B
2.	C	6.	B	10.	B	14.	D
3.	D	7.	B	11.	C	15.	D
4.	B	8.	D	12.	C	16.	B

NICKNAMES:

A Seleção —————— Brazil

Black Stars —————— Ghana

Clockwork Orange —— Netherlands

The Dragons —————— Wales

Die Mannschaft ———— Germany

Indomitable Lions —— Cameroon

La Albiceleste ———— Argentina

Lions of Teranga ———— Senegal

Socceroos —————— Australia

Taegeuk Warriors —— South Korea

The Three Lions ———— England

DRIBBLE CHALLENGE:

Answer: Player B

WHERE IN THE WORLD:

A. Canada
B. Mexico
C. Ecuador
D. Argentina
E. Denmark

F. Belgium
G. Portugal
H. Tunisia
I. Ghana
J. Iran

K. Qatar
L. Japan
M. Australia

THE LANGUAGE OF FOOTBALL:

1.	Shoot	5.	Corner	9.	Own Goal
2.	Penalty	6.	Throw In	10.	Red Card
3.	Offside	7.	Referee		
4.	Free Kick	8.	Striker		

SPOT THE DIFFERENCE:

ANAGRAMS:

1.	Harry Kane	6.	Kevin de Bruyne
2.	Cristiano Ronaldo	7.	Sadio Mané
3.	Kylian Mbappé	8.	Christian Pulisic
4.	Robert Lewandowski	9.	Son Heung-min
5.	Lionel Messi	10.	Declan Rice